While the Music Lasts
A Novel

*For Ann and Dick —
With best wishes —
Susan Frost*

Susan K. Frost

TRAFFORD
PUBLISHING

© Copyright 2006 Susan K. Frost.
All rights reserved. No part of this publication may be reproduced, stored in a retrieval system, or transmitted, in any form or by any means, electronic, mechanical, photocopying, recording, or otherwise, without the written prior permission of the author.

Note for Librarians: A cataloguing record for this book is available from Library and Archives Canada at www.collectionscanada.ca/amicus/index-e.html
ISBN 1-4251-0142-9

Printed in Victoria, BC, Canada. Printed on paper with minimum 30% recycled fibre.
Trafford's print shop runs on "green energy" from solar, wind and other environmentally-friendly power sources.

Offices in Canada, USA, Ireland and UK

Book sales for North America and international:
Trafford Publishing, 6E–2333 Government St.,
Victoria, BC V8T 4P4 CANADA
phone 250 383 6864 (toll-free 1 888 232 4444)
fax 250 383 6804; email to orders@trafford.com

Book sales in Europe:
Trafford Publishing (UK) Limited, 9 Park End Street, 2nd Floor
Oxford, UK OX1 1HH UNITED KINGDOM
phone +44 (0)1865 722 113 (local rate 0845 230 9601)
facsimile +44 (0)1865 722 868; info.uk@trafford.com

Order online at:
trafford.com/06-1899

10 9 8 7 6 5 4 3 2

The Blessed Damozel
by
Dante Gabriel Rossetti

In memory of my parents

and for

Jerry, James and Holly

PRELUDE

I said to my soul, be still, and wait without hope
For hope would be hope for the wrong thing; wait without love
For love would be love of the wrong thing; there is yet faith
But the faith and the love and the hope are all in the waiting.
Wait without thought, for you are not ready for thought:
So the darkness shall be the light, and the stillness the dancing.

> T. S. Eliot
> East Coker
> *Four Quartets*

WHILE THE MUSIC LASTS

The deed, as they say, was done and there was nothing Isabel could do to take it back. More and more she questioned the wisdom and the morality of her decision. When she conceived the idea she had told herself that it was not only correct but selfless and loving. Any doubts had been, she now saw, ruthlessly suppressed. But they had not been vanquished, and, as if emboldened by their survival, they now resurfaced with a vigor that left her weak with remorse. She knew that her actions were selfish in the extreme.

She had been standing by the window watching, but not really seeing, the activity in the Grand Canal. Now the midday sun was so bright that it hurt her eyes, and she turned to face the room. She had asked for elegance and, yes, in halting Italian, even for romance… a romantic room. They had done their best to accommodate her.

The hotel was once the luxurious palazzo of a fifteenth-century count. She assumed that her corner room, with its view of the Basilica of Santa Maria Della Salute, was one subdivision of the partego, the largest room on the piano nobile. Venetian artistry was spread in a panoply within the confines of her room's four walls. Her eyes traveled from the Rococo bed to the swelling bombé chest in front of her, its pale drawers decorated with hand-painted flowers. To her right she saw the gilt pier mirror and a few chairs upholstered in their various silks and damasks. Crowning everything was an enormous Murano glass chandelier.

She tried to focus intently on each item as if it were on display in a museum. She recognized this was a strategy to try to keep her mind occupied and her thoughts from admitting that there was an incessant drumbeat in her head. Feeling feverish, she went into the handsome marble bathroom and turned on the cold faucet of the wash basin.

With her eyes closed and her head bent close to the tap, she repeatedly cupped her hands full of the cool water and brought it up to splash and trickle down her face.

Returning to her bedroom, she lay languidly on top of the heavy red and gold brocade bedspread and, stretching out her arms, absently let her fingers trace the intricate pattern of its rich gold threads. Eventually, pulling down one corner of the spread, she allowed her cheek to rest on the cool cotton pillow beneath.

This was her third trip to Europe. Why, each time, had death or illness been central to her experience?

She let her mind drift back to that first transatlantic flight when she was just fourteen. Twenty-five years had passed, but she remembered every detail with amazing clarity:

The sun was just beginning to rise as their plane touched down at the Madrid airport. There was a flurry of claiming luggage, standing in lines and clearing customs.

By the time they were in a cab on the way to the hotel, Isabel had very nearly decided that she did not like Europe. The light on the buildings and on the streets seemed somehow distorted, and everything looked as though she were viewing it through a defective glass.

At the hotel they were told that their rooms were not yet ready and that they would have to wait in the lobby. They sat for what seemed like hours. In addition to the peculiar appearance of her surroundings, her stomach was signaling first hunger, then nausea. Her skin, always pale and lightly freckled beneath her lustrous red hair, became paler still. Her mother noticed.

"Darling, are you all right?"

"Jet lag," her father said, "a few hours sleep and you'll be fine." He always seemed to have an uncanny ability to define a problem and solve it succinctly.

Her mother went to the reception desk, smiled and said in a firm voice, "My daughter feels ill. She needs to lie down. I wonder if you can help me?"

When Isabel finally reached her room, she threw herself on the bed without bothering to turn it down.

Soon, far too soon, Isabel's mother, Cecily, was shaking her gently. "Time to wake up, sweetheart. If you sleep all day, you won't sleep tonight. And, besides, your father has bought tickets for the bullfight. He says we have really good seats, on the shady side and down close to the action."

Isabel groaned, "No, please, I'm too tired. You go and leave me here."

But her mother was insistent, "We can't leave you alone here, darling."

In the cab on the way to the corrida de toros, Isabel's father, David, explained what they would see. The precision and care he used in his work as an engineer extended to most aspects of his life. It was, he thought, a duty to research and prepare for an event, and he could be found with his head buried in volumes as diverse as the *Encyclopaedia Britannica*, the OED and obscure scholarly journals. On the plane to Madrid, he had finished reading Ernest Hemingway's *Death in the Afternoon*.

"Isabel," he said, "the bullfight begins with a procession of the cuadrillas who are the matador's attendants. You will be able to tell the matadors by their gold embroidery. No one else is allowed to wear that gold. The matador doesn't perform alone until the end when he makes the kill. That is called the Hour of Truth. Before this happens, his helpers on horseback place the banderillas, which are long sticks with barbs on the end. These both enrage and weaken the bull. And, by the way, the bulls aren't like those you would see on an ordinary farm. They are bred to be especially vicious and to attack without any provocation. When they are yearlings, they are tested for ferocity in the countryside. A number of them don't make it to the ring.

Some people think that the matadors use red capes because the color red makes the bull angrier, but that's not true. Bulls are color blind. The color red is used to keep the spattered blood from being too visible."

"Really?" Isabel's mother interjected. "That sounds positively gruesome!"

"It's a huge spectacle which began in this country. Its roots go back to four hundred something B.C."

The cab stopped outside the bull ring. The day was sunny with only small wisps of clouds. They found their seats that were, indeed, excellent. The large arena seemed full to capacity, and the crowd was expectant and enthusiastic.

"This really is amazing," Isabel thought. She was beginning to warm up to the idea of being in Europe.

The procession began with the entry of two aquaciles on horseback followed by the matadors in their brief jackets and skintight pants. They wore small black hats and black slippers, and Isabel was aware of a profusion of satin, silk and lace and pinkish-red stockings. Bandilleros and picadors followed in their turn as the dignified parade slowly crossed the ring. The mayor threw down the keys to the bull pens. Some participants left the arena while others positioned themselves for the fight.

The crowd gave a loud roar as the first bull was released. He was a magnificent specimen, sleek and muscular, and the people obviously believed him a worthy opponent for the matador. But Isabel thought she detected a slight

WHILE THE MUSIC LASTS

hesitancy in his pace. He seemed confused by the noise and the bright sunlight as though he had been thrust into the arena from some dark, familiar place and could not find his bearings.

The initial passes were not a success. The bull did not want to charge and made only a few half-hearted attempts after the cape had been waved in front of him repeatedly. A mounted picador, his horse well padded and protected against a possible goring, passed close to the bull to place a pair of barbed banderillas in its neck. As the pikes found their mark, the bull fell down. It slowly struggled back to its feet, and when it was once again upright, another pair of banderillas was placed. The result was the same. After its second fall, the bull took a fair amount of time getting up and seemed unsteady on its feet. It showed no interest in its tormentors but wobbled over to just below where Isabel and her parents were sitting. The crowd grew hushed. Isabel's father was swearing under his breath. The bull raised its head and Isabel looked directly into its large brown eyes. She began to tremble and felt like screaming but, as in a nightmare, she was incapable of making a sound.

Her mother stood and said firmly "That's enough. We're leaving."

When Isabel reached her room, she fell on her bed and began sobbing into her pillow. "I hated it! It was just horrible... that poor bull! How can people be so cruel?"

Isabel's mother came over, sat beside her and stroked her head. "I'm terribly sorry you had to witness that," she said. "I can't imagine what your father and I were thinking. It was ghastly."

She continued stroking Isabel's forehead, and, minutes later, as Isabel's sobs were beginning to subside, she asked the question that had, over a period of many years, become a ritual between them. It began when Isabel was very young and suffered night terrors. Unable to wake Isabel fully, Cecily would carry her around the apartment, pointing out various objects and trying to get her to focus on something to help her emerge from her terrified stupor. But, despite her best efforts, Isabel's screams usually continued unabated for some time.

One day, a possible solution to this problem presented itself in the form of an old painting Cecily found stuck behind two chairs at a tag sale. The painting was far from great art - it was, in fact, an example of the nineteenth century's often inordinate sentimentality; but it had quite a nice gilt frame and Cecily, though she had often been teased about her penchant for things overly romantic, nevertheless liked the depiction of a young woman sitting in a gondola being rowed down the Grand Canal in Venice. The woman could be seen only in profile from the back. What Cecily found particularly appealing was that the woman had long, flowing red hair and a pale porcelain complexion not unlike Cecily's own. For some time, Cecily had compared her own skin tone favorably with that of Amelie Avegno Gautreau, the subject of Sargent's painting "Madame X". A copy of that painting had hung in her parents' dining room since she was very young. Cecily, knowing that this coloring had also been passed on to Isabel, was certain that Isabel would, as she matured, enjoy looking at this picture of an unknown woman in Venice. Even with her lack of sophisticated knowledge of art, Cecily knew that the tag sale painting was hardly the equivalent of a Sargent. But rationalizing the purchase as being primarily for her daughter's well-being, the painting was taken home that same afternoon and duly installed at the foot of Isabel's crib. Cecily pointed to the picture often and told Isabel that someday, when she grew older, she would resemble the lady in the gondola. Now, when the night terrors came and later, when Isabel was very upset for some reason, Cecily had a cure. She would lift Isabel out of her crib, hold her up to the painting and suggest that they "go into the picture." The gondolier had his back to the viewer so they could imagine him singing jolly songs or soft lullabies (always provided by Cecily) and, rarely, it was decided that he would not sing at all. This game was so familiar to both of them that they could now play it even in the absence of the painting – so vivid was the picture in their imaginations.

Cecily thought the moments after the bullfight might be an excellent time for an imaginary trip to Venice; so she said very softly, "Would you like to go into the picture?"

Isabel believed that she was getting too old for such nonsense, but she knew her mother was simply trying to comfort her and, after a brief hesitation, she said yes.

"Is the gondolier singing today?" Cecily asked.

A "No, he's not" from Isabel meant that calming her would take some time. But a "Yes, he's singing 'O Sole Mio'" meant that Isabel was ready to continue with the charade.

Speaking softly, once again, Cecily asked, "And you, are you now the girl in the boat?"

"Yes."

"What are you feeling?"

"I'm feeling a little better."

"Are you looking at the beautiful palazzos on either side of the canal? Do you see how the afternoon sun strikes some of the windows?"

"Yes."

"And how is the water today? Are you in jostling waves in the wake of a larger boat?"

"No, the water is much calmer and I'm just floating."

"What do you want to do now?"

"I want to lean back against the red velvet cushion and close my eyes and listen to the music."

"This gondolier has a good voice?"

"A wonderful voice."

Gradually, the scenes in the bullring and Isabel's pity for the hapless bull were replaced by the gentle rocking of the gondola and the sweet song of the gondolier, and, finally allowing exhaustion to have its way, Isabel fell into a deep, restorative sleep.

Cecily whispered to David, "It would be a shame to wake her for dinner. If she is hungry in the night, we can order room service, but I think, as strenuous as this day has been, she could well sleep straight through until morning."

Isabel slept not only until morning but until noon of the next day. Even then, she was in no hurry to get up, and she yawned and stretched several times before taking a leisurely shower. She decided to wear a cotton dress and, on her way out the door, she stopped and went back for her wide-brimmed straw hat. She would need to protect her fair complexion from the Spanish sun. Knocking on her parents' door, she gave them each a hug when they opened it and then, remembering how long it had been since she had eaten, proceeded to tell them she was famished.

Lunch in the hotel's open-air rooftop restaurant began auspiciously. It was a day of gentle breezes. In the clear light beneath the azure sky, they were able to see for miles across the tops of the city's buildings.

Tables with starched, white cloths and napkins were

set in the shade of a pergola. Its green vines and an abundance of flowers in colorful pots were intended to make the patrons feel they were in a garden. Isabel heard the sounds of silverware on china and caught snatches of conversations from adjacent tables.

The family to the left, parents with a small boy of about four or five, spoke quietly in British accents. Isabel overheard them discussing the previous afternoon's bullfight. The small boy seemed enthralled by Isabel. She believed it might have something to do with the fact that they shared the same coloring. His auburn hair framed a face full of freckles, and he stared at her intently with handsome green eyes. She thought him adorable, and when she smiled at him, he smiled back. His parents were too engrossed in their conversation to notice.

The first course consisted of a cold tomato soup which her parents told her was called gazpacho. The waiter passed a tray of little bowls containing chopped green peppers, olives, onions, tomatoes and hard-boiled eggs to sprinkle over the soup. Isabel tasted the soup tentatively before commenting that she liked it.

On the table, a glass pitcher filled with burgundy, club soda and sundry liqueurs had quartered oranges, lemons and ice floating in it.

"Would you like just a taste of this sangria?" her mother asked.

Isabel nodded and said, "Yes, please."

She ate every morsel of something that was called paella, a rice dish with seafood and saffron. Isabel's parents suggested flan custards for dessert. As they were finishing their meal, the little boy at the adjacent table stood and came over to Isabel.

"Hello," he said. "What's your name?"

WHILE THE MUSIC LASTS

Before she had a chance to answer, his parents were apologizing for the intrusion. Everyone seemed to speak at once before there was a sudden lull and silence. To bridge this, the child's father spoke to Isabel, saying with a smile, "You're the little lady who was so upset by the bullfight, aren't you?"

Isabel's father answered for her. "We were all upset," he said.

The man's wife said, "Yes, well, the first fight was really bad, hardly a fight at all, actually. But it wasn't so bad after the first one. The third bull tested the matador for quite a long time, and we could get a sense of what the spectacle is supposed to be."

Suddenly, the little boy said, in his loud, clear child's voice, "Why is the fight bad?"

His parents shushed him but he persisted, "Why is it bad, Daddy, why?"

"Because the bull dies, Christopher." His father said.

Christopher was satisfied for a few moments and then, with the understandable self-absorption of the young, said, "I won't die, will I?"

"No," his mother replied, "not for a very long time."

"I'll never die!" Christopher said emphatically.

"Well, yes, you will, son," his father spoke quietly. "We all die someday."

"No!" Christopher said, his voice rising to a heartbroken wail. "I don't want to die!"

Conversation in the restaurant ceased as everyone turned to look at the child. His mother swept him up in her arms and carried him out as his father quickly paid the bill.

Isabel's mother shook her head and said softly, "I imagine it's particularly hard to confront mortality at such a tender age."

"Mortality... a tender age..." Now, all these years later, Isabel could hear her mother's voice as clearly as though she were sitting beside her. Then, abruptly, there was another voice, an ugly, shrill voice from when she was very young.

"You can't let them run your life. Children will, you know, if you let them. You should find someone to watch her so you can get away and have time for yourself. Children can be so damned draining. I'm always exhausted if I'm around them too long."

Later, she had asked, "Mummy, am I draining?"

"What do you mean, darling?"

"Your friend said children are draining."

"Oh, no, that's absolute rubbish. Some people think only about themselves and have nothing left over for anyone else."

"Am I around you too much?"

Her mother had taken Isabel's face between her hands and looked directly into her eyes. "Of course not, my angel. You are the best thing that ever happened to me. You must never forget that."

Now, actually in Venice, Isabel continued to look around her hotel room until she heard a commotion beneath her window. Curious, she rose from the bed and looked out. A gondolier and a man in a small power boat were gesticulating angrily. Isabel could not understand what had transpired, but each of the men was obviously eager to have the last word.

WHILE THE MUSIC LASTS

Further out in the canal, two gondolas were full of school children paddling. Each boat had an adult sitting in a sort of coxswain's seat, supervising the children's progress. Isabel wondered if this were the Venetian equivalent of a gym class.

Returning to the bed, she carefully replaced the bedspread over the pillow, so that the room was once again as immaculate as the maid had left it. She recalled her mother's teaching her how to make a bed and how to miter the corners neatly.

Suddenly, Isabel wanted her mother with all of the aching need of a child. She wanted to bury her face in her mother's neck and smell the scent of her familiar perfume. She wanted to cry while her mother held her in her arms and comforted her. She wanted the safety of being with the one person who had always put her first and whom she could trust implicitly. She longed for her mother's reassurance. But she knew her mother could never have approved of what she was doing now because it was not only selfish, it was unforgivable.

PART ONE

A host of things I take on trust; I take

The Nightingales on trust, for few and far

Between those actual summer moments are

When I have heard what melody they make.

Christina Rossetti

"Later Life"

WHILE THE MUSIC LASTS

Isabel was a city child during the school year. Her parents owned an apartment on the upper East Side of Manhattan. When she was young she went to the day school at the Church of the Heavenly Rest. In second grade she had been given the honor of playing the Virgin Mary in the Christmas pageant. What she remembered most about that occasion was that she had been jealous of the girl who had the part of the Angel Gabriel; this girl was allowed to wear an elaborate, glittering gold costume while Mary was assigned a decidedly inferior plain, blue dress.

Isabel made friends easily and was often invited to birthday parties. At some of these, she noted that the elevators opened directly into her friends' apartments instead of into a common corridor like the one in her own building. At one party, she and the other guests hid behind massive brocade draperies in a long living room whose windows fronted the East River. She loved the anticipation of waiting to hear voices in the foyer, then jumping out and crying "Surprise! Happy birthday!"

Her parents' apartment had a view of the Chrysler Building. Isabel's room was on a court. On warm spring evenings, she could hear some child practicing the violin. The first notes of the "Star Spangled Banner" were played over and over because the sixth note was invariably off key. Isabel winced as the wrong note was continuously repeated. She herself had begun taking piano lessons at the suggestion of her mother. Usually obedient, Isabel would now and again balk at doing repetitious scales. She would start to fidget, and then, pushing herself away from the piano entirely, she would sigh heavily, saying, "I'm tired!"

Her mother then decided to enlist the aid of a good friend whom Isabel knew as "Aunt Catherine." Catherine

WHILE THE MUSIC LASTS

had graduated from Juilliard and continued her studies with a famous pianist in France. One afternoon she came to give Isabel a pep talk.

"I know scales can be terribly boring, darling, but they are important, believe me. The more you practice, the sooner you will be able to play really beautiful pieces. Your mother tells me you have a recital coming up soon. You must be excited about that. And we think it might be fun to go shopping for a new dress for you to wear. You will want to look especially pretty when you play for an audience, won't you?"

Isabel looked down. "It will be scary to play in front of people."

"Oh, my dear, when I was your age, someone told me something that has always helped me. She said 'Don't think of an audience as rows of people. Think of them as rows of cabbages!'"

Isabel laughed and said, "That's funny!" but she still looked a bit skeptical so Catherine continued, "And remember to take a deep breath before you start; that's a big help too. Now, dear, will you play your recital piece for me?"

Isabel obliged and Catherine applauded at the end.

"That was lovely. There is just one phrase you might do slightly differently." She came over to the piano to demonstrate. "It's better this way, isn't it?"

Catherine's visit had the desired effect. Isabel practiced diligently and, before long, she was accompanying her mother and Catherine on the promised shopping trip to choose a dress for the recital. Isabel tried on several designs, but the three of them kept coming back to a pale green velvet, which complimented her skin and eyes. Isabel decided to wear her hair up with a matching green bow.

The recital was a success, and Isabel played well although still with the tentativeness of a beginner; it would be years before she was able to follow her teacher's instruction to "relax and let the music flow through you."

Shortly after her own performance, Isabel learned that aiming too high as a concert pianist could be the cause of immense disappointment. Aunt Catherine was going to give a concert at Town Hall. Isabel was told she could stay up late that evening to attend, and she was very excited at the prospect. As the program began, Isabel felt very adult sitting in the audience, but as the concert neared completion, she leaned on her mother's arm and fell asleep.

The next day she heard her parents discussing the concert and the failure of the *New York Times* to review it in any meaningful way. Apparently there were a few lines saying something to the effect that "Miss Catherine Anderson played a concert at Town Hall to an appreciative audience of well-wishers." Isabel's mother was incensed. "That performance was the culmination of her whole life's work!"

Isabel's father was more philosophical. "Darling, all of us, all of her friends agree that she played beautifully. But you must remember that only a handful of artists possess talent important enough to be called great. And the newspaper is looking for distinction. The *Times* doesn't care how long or hard a person has worked."

Isabel spent her summers with her maternal grandparents. They lived in a small town in upstate New York. Its Front Street was comprised of numerous, grand mid-nineteenth-century houses whose large back lawns sloped down to the Susquehanna River. The area in which Isabel's grandparents lived was designated an historic district. Their home, a stately, vernacular red brick house, had abundant Georgian and Federal details. There was a grape arbor at the back with a stone bench inside. Isabel loved to sit there, feeling completely protected as she peered through the leaves at the lawn beyond. The gardener had planted a large, circular flower bed that could be enjoyed from the screened porch where Isabel and her grandparents had dinner on fine days. The bed was rimmed with primroses, Isabel's birth flower.

Her mother would bring her to her grandparents in June and stay a week or two before returning to the city, leaving Isabel to enjoy the benefits of fresh air, grass and flowers. Isabel was particularly fond of the pink roses that lined a path leading to the white barn. The barn had windows with red shutters and had once been a stable for horses and carriages but was now used for storage and as a garage.

One lovely June morning when she was four, her mother gave her a brightly striped, red-and-blue rubber ball. Isabel and Andrew, the little boy who lived in the stucco house next door, spent time playing with the ball, throwing it and catching it and running after it together until they were respectively called in for lunch. After the meal, Isabel and her mother and grandparents strolled out to the yard, and Isabel ran to retrieve her new ball that she had left at the edge of a flower bed. Carrying it in her right hand, she returned to her mother and took her mother's hand with her left. Her mother looked down indulgently and asked if she would like to walk to the end of the lawn to see the Susquehanna. As long as she could remember, Isabel had been warned not to go to the bank of the river without an adult. Her grandparents designated a certain tree as the boundary marker. She was allowed to go that far but no farther. This usually forbidden venture was a special treat and Isabel eagerly agreed. They stood together hand in hand watching the river as the current carried small pieces of debris and parts of branches into view and then quickly out of sight.

Suddenly, a squirrel bounded in front of them and ran up a tree to their right. Startled, Isabel dropped the ball. It bounced twice and went rolling down the bank into the river. Isabel let go of her mother's hand and moved to follow the ball. Her mother shrieked, "No!" and roughly grabbed her. Isabel had never heard her mother make such a sound and she began to cry. Her mother tried to comfort her, immediately saying, "I'll buy you another one." But it was not the loss of the ball so much as the horror in her mother's voice that made Isabel inconsolable. She associated that horror with the river.

Andrew heard Isabel crying and came over to ask her to play in his yard. "We can even play house if you want to," he said. He disliked being the "daddy" to Isabel's baby dolls, but he hated to see her upset. After a few minutes, Isabel agreed. She thought Andrew's house was even more beautiful than her grandparents' home and she loved to go there. The house, of creamy stucco, had an Italianate cornice and a columned Greek Revival porch. Centered directly above this front porch was a Palladian window through which, at night, shone the light from a very large Waterford crystal chandelier. This light fascinated Isabel, and she would ask her grandparents to take her out at twilight to see it.

Andrew's parents had a lovely rectangular swimming pool in their back garden. Later that summer, they taught Andrew to swim and offered to teach Isabel. But when her grandmother took her over, Isabel saw something in the deep end of the pool and she hung back. Andrew's father dove in and brought up a rabbit that had fallen into the water and drowned. Isabel wanted nothing to do with the pool, and when Andrew tried to pull her down the steps, she became hysterical. The idea of swimming lessons had to be abandoned.

―――

When she was older, Isabel attended the Chapin School. There she wore a uniform, learned her weekly Bible verses by heart, studied penmanship, which gave her an exquisite hand she would retain throughout her life, and dealt with the required subjects of English, French, history, geography and math. She showed particular ability in French and extra-curricular ability in music. She was becoming an accomplished pianist, and she had a light, lyric soprano voice that blended well in the chorus of girls' voices singing hymns in assembly. She very much enjoyed the majestic melody of the hymn "Jerusalem," although she had no idea what the words meant. The phrases "arrows of desire" and "building Jerusalem in England's green and pleasant land" were beyond her ken. She wondered why anyone would want to build a middle-eastern city in England.

When the time came, she and many of her classmates studied for and experienced the rite of Confirmation in the Episcopal Church. Isabel loved the liturgy; the rich cadences in the *Book of Common Prayer* were deeply satisfying to her. She was not always sure of their meaning, but the format of the priest making a statement followed by a response of the congregation in unison made her feel part of a larger whole, and she enjoyed the sense of belonging.

If a sermon bored her, Isabel let her attention wander to the jeweled tones of the stained glass windows as the sun shone through them illuminating stories from the Bible. She was awed by the majesty of the organ, and she could never quite understand why, at the end of services, while the organist was still playing Bach, people would talk with each other instead of listening to the waves of sound that, as they washed over her, gave her goose bumps. She very much hoped to learn to play the organ one day.

Isabel gave no thought to the gold cross on the altar because, as far as she could remember, it had always been there. She also accepted unquestioningly the teaching that Christ died on the cross for the sins of mankind and the reference to Him as the sacrificial "Lamb of God." It was many years later before she understood the horrific agony of crucifixion and began to question how an all-merciful God could demand such suffering as an expiation.

When Isabel graduated near the top of her class and was accepted at Bryn Mawr, Smith College, and Swarthmore College, she and her parents held a family conference. Her mother was a graduate of Bryn Mawr and tried to steer her daughter in that direction.

"I had four such marvelous years there. I'm sure you would too."

"But, Mother, I…"

"Perhaps we could start a tradition. Someday you might have a daughter who would like to go there as well…"

"Mother, I know it's a wonderful college. But I have been in girls' schools all my life, and I want to start meeting some boys. Swarthmore is coeducational, and I'm really leaning toward that right now."

"Swarthmore is a fine school too," Isabel's father interjected.

WHILE THE MUSIC LASTS

Isabel's mother gave in gracefully. "All right, darling. If you think you'll be happier there, Swarthmore it is."

As high school commencement neared, Isabel's parents asked if there were anything in particular she would like to have as a graduation gift. Isabel had been anticipating this question and knew what her answer would be.

"Mother, for as long as I can remember, you and I have been making imaginary excursions in that painted gondola. I want to go to Venice, see the sights and ride down the Grand Canal in a real gondola!"

Isabel's mother beamed her approval. "Why, of course! That's a wonderful idea, and I wish your dad and I had thought of it and surprised you with the tickets! But, actually, it's nice you mentioned it this early; now we'll have time to go to the library and take out some books to help you choose what you would most like to see. Venice has so many fascinating places…. We won't be there long enough to see them all but we can certainly take in most of the highlights. This is really exciting!" She leaned over and gave Isabel a hug.

Isabel's father asked when they would go and unofficially put himself in charge of making all of the arrangements.

Cecily and Isabel looked at each other and both started to speak.

Cecily said, "I think toward the end of the summer…"

Isabel added, "I wouldn't want to miss spending most of the summer with my grand…"

The two women laughed as they instantly agreed that the best time to go would be at the beginning of August after their annual visit to upstate New York.

David smiled at his wife and daughter. "All right, ladies," he said. "Good idea."

PART TWO

I cannot live with you
It would be Life -
And life is over there -
Behind the Shelf

The sexton keeps the Key to -
Putting up
Our Life - His Porcelain
Like a Cup -

Discarded of the Housewife -
Quaint – or Broke -
A newer Sevres pleases -
Old Ones crack.

Emily Dickinson

WHILE THE MUSIC LASTS

As the summer after graduation from preparatory school began, Isabel felt a sense of real elation. She had been class salutatorian, and she was eagerly looking forward to the start of college in the fall. She had already decided that she would probably major in French and hoped to spend her junior year at the Swarthmore program in Grenoble. Packing to go to her grandparents, she included a French dictionary, an advanced grammar book and several novels in French. She planned to study these during the summer to help her with the advanced placement tests in September.

Two days before she was supposed to leave, she received a note from Andrew. "There will be a surprise when you get here. Come soon! See you. - Andy."

It rained at the end of May and during the first few days of June; but on the day of their arrival, the showers were over by noon and Isabel's grandparents, her beloved Nana and Grandpapa, were enjoying the afternoon sun as they looked out the window waiting for their daughter and Isabel to arrive. When the car pulled up, they came down the stairs to meet them exclaiming, "Here you are at last!"

Isabel's Nana appeared stately in a soft floral print dress, her white hair piled high with combs. She was wearing a single strand of pearls. Isabel's Grandpapa, tall, lanky, his once red hair fading now to grey, smiled with pleasure. His side of the family was responsible for the red hair that had been passed down to Isabel and her mother. Although he had hated his own auburn mop when he was a boy because it led to teasing and nicknames like "Red" and "Carrot Top," he was proud of how becoming the color was on his daughter and granddaughter. Like him, they were tall and thin with alabaster skin and striking green eyes. They sometimes reminded him of two, fragile, Dresden china figurines.

Isabel threw herself into her grandparents' waiting arms. Her mother followed closely behind carrying a suitcase.

"Cecily, let me have that. It's too heavy for you," Grandpapa said. "I'll bring up the rest of your things."

Cecily didn't object. "Oh, thanks, Dad, " she said. "I must be out of shape because it really isn't that heavy."

After unpacking, Isabel's mother put her things in what had been her childhood room while Isabel settled into the room across the hall; they emerged and started down the long staircase together. Isabel said, "I love this house so much. I even have dreams about it sometimes. Aren't we lucky it has been in the family going back so many years – to times before we were even born?"

Cecily smiled, "Yes, we're very fortunate," she said. "It's becoming rare for houses to remain in the same families for generations these days. The conventional wisdom is that America is a country on the move."

"Who is moving?" Nana asked, holding out two glasses of iced tea to them as they entered the screened porch.

"No one is, Mother" Cecily replied. "We were just congratulating ourselves on the fact that this house has been here and in our family for such a long time."

Nana smiled. "Yes, I'd love to know what these walls have seen and heard over the past one hundred and fifty years!"

"I should go next door to see Andrew," Isabel said. "He wrote that he has a surprise for me."

"He's not home yet. The whole family has gone off to Binghamton to do some errands. You'll see them this evening. They've invited all of us over for dinner."

"How very thoughtful of them!" Isabel's mother

exclaimed.

"Do have a cookie, dear," Isabel's grandmother urged her daughter. "I know they are your favorites and I made them this morning."

"Thanks, Mother. I'm sure they're wonderful, as always, but I'm just not very hungry."

"I hope you're not dieting, dear. You are already too thin and you have been working too hard again, I'm afraid. You never have been able to say no when someone wants you to head a charity drive. You took on a new one just recently, didn't you?"

"Yes, but I..."

"What is it this time?"

"We are trying to help the homeless. There aren't enough shelters and the few there are desperately need renovating. Many of the needy are mentally ill. It makes me angry that in a country as wealthy as ours, we allow sick people to lie on the sidewalks... Oh, I'm sorry. Here I am, up on my soapbox preaching again."

"No, what you are doing is important," Isabel's grandfather replied. "But we know how much of yourself you put into any project you take on."

"I'm just trying to do my bit. But I have to admit that I've been feeling unusually tired lately. In fact, I thought I might extend my stay here an extra week this year - if you both won't mind putting up with me that long."

"If it were up to me," Isabel's grandfather smiled, "you would stay the entire summer!"

It was just past five thirty in the afternoon and Isabel's mother seemed in a reflective mood as they sat on the porch waiting until it was time to walk next door for dinner.

"Isn't it a matter of course," she said, "that the world

seemed most beautiful when we were children? Perhaps it's because everything was so new to us then. I remember summer evenings here when the scent of flowers, the late daylight and the long shadows on the lawn were some of the loveliest things imaginable. At the time I had no way of knowing that, as an adult, I would never be able to experience evening in quite the same way again."

"I remember how rebellious you were at having to go to bed while it was still daylight," Isabel's grandmother said.

"Yes, I would lie in the nursery watching the dotted Swiss curtains blow in the breeze from the open window and make plans to grow up and do exactly as I pleased. I'm afraid I wished away my innocence without any true appreciation of it."

"That's rather poetic," Isabel's grandfather said. "Have you been reading Wordsworth: intimations of immortality, trailing clouds of glory and all that sort of thing?"

"No," Cecily smiled. "I really don't know what started me thinking about my childhood."

"Well, this has been a particularly pleasant day, dear," Isabel's grandmother said. "Perhaps it jogged some memories."

"Do you know one of the times I remember best? I had been really sick with the measles -"

"You nearly died with the measles," Isabel's grandfather interjected. "Thank God they have a vaccine now."

"Yes, but I was better and it was a perfect, warm day and you said that, if I had no fever, mother could take me out for a drive. After you put the thermometer in my mouth and left the room, I waited until it registered normal on the red line then took it out of my mouth until I heard you coming back. I was desperate to go out after three weeks of being in bed. So mother and I drove out to the country, and we stopped and picked some Queen Anne's Lace along the side of the road. Do you remember that?"

"Yes, it was so good to have you well again and able to go out. But I didn't realize at the time that it was under false pretences, you wicked girl!" Nana smiled. "I remember how beautiful that day was. I'm reminded of Emily Dickinson's poem where she speaks of 'a sea of summer air.' I've always liked that metaphor."

"Precisely!" Cecily said, "and that is exactly what today has been: 'a sea of summer air.' Dickinson's ability to express it in such terms probably means that the great poets never lose their capacity to see as a child sees - the way the rest of us do."

"I don't think you have lost yours, Mother," Isabel said, putting her arm around her mother's waist as they all rose to go to dinner.

"Oh, but I have, darling," her mother replied, laughing. "I have!"

Andrew was waiting for them and flung open the door as they came up the walk. They stepped into the large entrance hall and felt the familiar welcoming splendor of the house. There was a circular staircase in front of them, its well illuminated by the chandelier on the second floor. The long living room to the right had dark green velvet portieres in the doorway and, through these, they glimpsed the matching green carpet and the Federal mirror above a console table between the tall front windows. The long draperies had rose and lavender flowers on a creamy ground. Beyond the sofa was a Steinway piano. Dark oil portraits of nineteenth century ancestors hung on the walls.

Isabel started into this room, but Andrew directed her toward the back of the house.

"They're all in the conservatory," he said, leading her past the stairway.

Andrew's family, sitting in white wicker chairs surrounded by a profusion of plants and hanging flower baskets, rose to greet them. There were many hugs and much laughter. Isabel was quickly aware of a boy of about Andrew's age who was standing awkwardly next to Andrew's mother. Isabel had never seen him before. He had tousled dark brown hair that looked as if it had gone its own curly direction despite his best efforts with a comb. His nose was a bit too large for his face and he had handsome, deep-set, dark eyes that registered the unease of someone who feels momentarily out of place.

"This," said Andrew, with a note of triumph in his voice, "is Jean-Marc Mabille. He's the surprise!"

Jean-Marc shook Isabel's hand and said, "How do you do?" in a very French accent.

Andrew, seeing Isabel's incomprehension, hurried to explain. "Remember, I spent last summer in France living with a family in Fontainebleau trying to improve my French? Well, Jean-Marc is the eldest son in that family, and, this year, he will be spending the summer here hoping to learn more English.

"We thought that we might set up some informal study sessions - maybe speaking English in the mornings and French in the afternoons. At any rate, you are welcome to join us, Isabel!"

Everyone spoke at once.

Isabel's mother exclaimed, "What a marvelous opportunity!"

Isabel said, "Andy, what a great surprise!"

As the general hubbub subsided, Jean-Marc was quiet. Seeing this, Isabel went up to him and rested her hand

WHILE THE MUSIC LASTS

lightly on his arm saying "Je vais bien, merci. Comment allez-vous?"

Jean-Marc relaxed and offered Isabel a seat beside him. They fell into easy conversation with Isabel speaking French and Jean-Marc answering in English. This gradually grew into a pattern they would pursue throughout the summer, encouraging each other and correcting each other as the need arose.

To remind Jean-Marc of home, Andrew's family planned a French dinner, beginning with escargots. There was warm French bread and the entrée was a daube of beef and garlic. The meal ended with a dessert of raspberry sherbet and madeleines made from a recipe Jean-Marc's mother had sent over with him, tucked in a pocket of his suitcase.

"This is delightful!" Isabel's grandfather said. "And, Jean-Marc, I'm sure you know this cake has a famous literary connotation – "

Jean-Marc smiled. "You are thinking of Proust and his madeleine."

"I must admit I found *À la Recherche du Temps Perdu* awfully hard going at first - and I was reading it in English translation."

Jean-Marc laughed. "I'm glad you like the cake. I also find Proust difficult - even in French," he added, smiling again.

"And you live in Fontainebleau?"

"My family - they have a house in Fontainebleau for the summer."

"A summer house?" Isabel asked.

"Yes, yes a summer house. We live in Paris all of the other times."

"You live in Paris during the rest of the year," Isabel

stated softly in a tone of voice conveying to Jean-Marc that what he had said was correct but that her expression was closer to the English conversational norm.

"Yes, during the rest of the year," he repeated after her. "My father, he has a big export business. He does much business with America. He says I will help him very much when I learn English more good – no - I mean, better."

"Ah," Isabel said smiling and nodding her approval at his use of the word "better," "excellent."

Jean-Marc beamed at her. "Thank you," he said.

After dinner, Andrew and his parents prevailed on Isabel to perform something on the piano.

"We haven't heard you play in such a long time. You have studied for so many years now that you are an accomplished pianist."

Isabel blushed. "I'm not, really."

"Please let us hear something."

Isabel had long loved their Steinway Model B, a size between a baby grand and a concert grand. It had a depth and richness of tone unlike any other piano she had played. So, after a bit more coaxing, she obliged.

Casting a meaningful glance at Jean-Marc, she said, "This is to honor your French guest," and began with "Clair de Lune." After a Chopin étude, she ended with Liszt's "Un Sospiro," which was a particular favorite of hers. When everyone applauded enthusiastically, Isabel smiled modestly and thanked them.

The party ended near midnight and Isabel and her family walked home in high spirits. Isabel found it hard to fall asleep in what was now a combination study and guest room. She heard the hall clock strike two, turned on her light, found her French copy of Stendhal's *Le Rouge et le Noir* and was plumping up her pillows before starting to

WHILE THE MUSIC LASTS

read when she heard someone come out of the bathroom and muffled voices outside her door. She got up and peered into the dim hallway. Her mother and grandmother were whispering together.

"What is it?" she asked.

"Your mother is sick. She has a bad case of indigestion, and I've given her something to settle her stomach," her grandmother answered.

"It must have been the snails," Cecily said. "I'm sorry if I woke you."

"I haven't been asleep yet. It was such a wonderful evening; I keep reliving it all in my head. But I'm terribly sorry you are sick. Can I help?"

"No, sweetheart, " Isabel's mother replied. "Go back to bed. I'm feeling better now, and we must all try to get some sleep!"

Isabel gave her mother a hug and said, "Good night. I hope you'll be all right." As she was falling asleep, she wondered if just one snail had gone bad, since she and her grandmother seemed fine. She hoped her grandfather and Andrew's family had managed to escape as well.

The entire household slept late the next morning. Brunch was on the screened porch where the table was set with a bright cloth patterned in red geraniums. Grandmother had brought out the informal green stoneware plates. There were cold cuts and corn bread, sweet pecan rolls and Eggs Benedict. In the center was a cut glass pitcher full of iced tea flavored with mint from the garden.

Isabel's grandfather was unusually quiet and Cecily asked, "Is everything all right, Dad?"

"Oh, yes," he replied. "I was just remembering what you said last evening about your childhood and I was thinking how parents try their best to shield their children from the ugly things in life."

"You did a fine job of protecting me," Isabel's mother said.

"My point, exactly," he replied, salting his eggs.

"Were you remembering something in particular?" Cecily questioned.

"I was thinking how little you ever knew about some of the tragedies that occurred in this town. You understood that I was kept out of the Korean War because of my slight heart murmur. But you never realized how many young men from here - men about my age - were soldiers and how many of them were killed."

"Speaking of war, " Isabel's grandmother said, "there was the little girl who was your friend when you were four or five, Rachel Lowenstein…"

"Yes, I remember her - but she moved away after awhile. Why do you mention her? What did she have to do with it?"

"Her grandparents and parents were refugees from Nazi Germany during World War II. Her mother told me that many in their families were killed in the death camps."

"My God!" Cecily exclaimed. "I never knew that! When I was small, the only thing I ever remember hearing you say about World War II was that there were food shortages and rationing and that some people frequented the black market. In my mind, I saw this grocery store draped all in black with black lettering on the windows, and I thought only bad people went there!"

That afternoon the French and English lessons began in earnest. Isabel, Andrew and Jean-Marc went alternately to each other's houses and often took breaks for iced tea and cookies around three o'clock. Later in the week, when it was Isabel's turn to entertain, her grandparents joined them for tea. Her grandmother had made fresh brownies that morning.

"These are delicious, Nana," Isabel said. Turning to Andrew she remarked, "Do you remember when we were little and that old Miss Murphy, your housekeeper, baked cakes and cookies? On nice days, she had the kitchen door and all of the windows open…"

Andrew broke in "Yes, which meant the scent of what was baking floated out to the yard… and, whenever we went and asked for just one cookie -"

"We would ask nicely, too," Isabel added.

"Yes, we remembered to say 'please,' but Miss Murphy always said no."

"Remember how she wore those long grey skirts with a rosary at her waist, and starched white blouses and had her hair pulled back tight in a bun?"

"Yes, she was always frowning, and she would lock the screen door so we couldn't come into the kitchen."

"But once, we saw a hole in the screen door," Isabel said, "and we went and got a broom out of the barn and stuck the handle through the hole and wiggled it around. And she got so mad, her face turned bright red!"

"As I recall," Isabel's grandmother said, "you were both punished for tormenting the poor woman."

"The worst part of that was having to go and say we were sorry," Isabel said.

"Because we weren't sorry!" Andrew agreed, laughing. "Not one bit!"

"You two were incorrigible!" Isabel's grandmother smiled indulgently.

WHILE THE MUSIC LASTS

"What you children failed to appreciate at the time was that Miss Murphy was a frustrated old maid," Isabel's grandfather remarked. "You were symbolic of what she could never have: a home and family of her own."

"Oh," Isabel's grandmother laughed, "you can't know that. Maybe she was one of the original feminists."

"Frustrated in love, more likely," he replied. "Helps to explain her sour disposition."

A few days later as the three language students were taking a break, drinking Cokes and lounging beside Andrew's pool, Jean-Marc suggested a swim before dinner. A flicker of fear passed over Isabel's face. Only someone who knew her well would have noticed it and Andrew did. He hastily intervened.

"Isabel doesn't swim," he said

"You don't swim?" Jean-Marc asked. "Why don't you swim?"

"I don't like the water," she said, embarrassed to have her phobia suddenly revealed.

Andrew came to the rescue. "She had a terrific scare when she was small, so she does not swim." He emphasized the last words in an attempt to convey to Jean-Marc that he should drop the subject.

Jean-Marc understood and said "I'm sorry, ma petite." He had begun using that endearment with her and she quite liked it.

"You couldn't have known," Isabel said, dropping her eyes.

Jean-Marc quickly lost his initial shyness and was soon regaling them in both French and English with stories of the wonders of Paris. After a time, Andrew began to resent what he believed to be Jean-Marc's boastfulness. Andrew, having been to Europe with his family and having spent a summer in France, had to admit that Paris was, indeed, superb, but he grew increasingly irritated as Jean–Marc not only never missed an opportunity to remind them of that fact but often made invidious comparisons to other European capitals as well.

Isabel was aware of the undercurrent between Andrew and Jean-Marc. Sometimes she noticed a fleeting look of amusement on Jean-Marc's face when Andrew stumbled on a French phrase or idiom. She wondered if Jean-Marc felt that he needed to compete with Andrew, if he saw him as a masculine rival for her attention. She knew such an assumption was absurd because her affection for Andrew had never been more than sisterly.

The days passed quickly. Isabel's mother returned to New York. June soon ended and they were in mid-July. The three congratulated each other on their linguistic prowess. Andrew noticed that Isabel was particularly attentive to Jean-Marc, that she would steal glances at him when he was looking elsewhere and was totally unaware. Then came the particularly hot and humid afternoon when Jean-Marc brazenly raised the forbidden subject. Looking directly at Isabel, Jean-Marc suddenly seemed full of determination. "The other day," he said, "when I looked out of my bedroom window, I saw you sunbathing in your garden. You were wearing a swimsuit."

"Yes," Isabel replied hesitantly.

"You own a swimsuit but you do not swim?" He asked, with a suggestion of irony in his voice.

Andrew started to speak, but Jean-Marc would not allow the interruption and went on as if Andrew were not there. His entire attention was focused on Isabel. "You do not swim because you are afraid. But together - you and

WHILE THE MUSIC LASTS

I – we are going to get over – I mean overcome - this fear. You will learn to swim and I will teach you. It is important to swim. It is not just a casual thing. It might mean your life someday."

Isabel said, "Oh, I can't," but Jean-Marc insisted.

"Yes, you can," he said. "We will go very slowly but you must learn. This is a child's fear and you are no longer a child. Now you will go, please, and put on the suit."

Caught in the midst of conflicting emotions, Isabel rose to obey.

Andrew, aware of her terror, was amazed.

Isabel failed to see the triumphant smile Jean-Marc flashed at Andrew as, ten minutes later, she started down the steps into the pool. Jean-Marc had bet Andrew that he could teach Isabel to swim. The bet had been a simple handshake, nothing more; but Andrew was chagrined that Jean-Marc was succeeding so easily at something he was certain would end in failure. Andrew found Jean-Marc's competitiveness irritating and he wondered why he found it necessary. Was Jean-Marc interested in Isabel and was he vying for her affection? This idea amused Andrew; he would have thought it was obvious that he and Isabel would never be more than the best of friends.

Jean-Marc, true to his word, led Isabel very slowly down the five steps into the shallow end of the pool where the water reached to her waist. He gave constant encouragement, saying, "Bon, bon, ma petite" and "Look at me; look only into my eyes - do not look at the water. Remember this is just a pool. It is not scary like the big river."

Isabel did as he said, focusing on his eyes, which were exultant and full of resolve.

"There, you see, " Jean-Marc said. "You are in the

pool and we will stay here. We will not go where it is deep. So you can stand at any time. It is okay?"

"Yes," Isabel said breathlessly, "it is okay."

"Now watch me," Jean-Marc said; "hold onto the side and kick with your legs straight."

When Isabel had accomplished this, Jean-Marc showed her how to hold her breath and move her arms. After a few false starts, Isabel managed a beginner's dog paddle. The fact that she was not only buoyant but that she could actually swim forward made Isabel giddy with elation and gratitude.

"Oh, Jean-Marc, thank you!" she said as he backed away, motioning her to swim toward him. When he reached the side and she was able to follow him, she stood up, took his face in her hands and kissed his cheek, whispering, "Merci beaucoup" into his ear. She could feel his strong, muscular arms around her waist as he gave her a hug, and they both laughed at the sheer joy of their accomplishment.

Looking back, Isabel knew that it was at that moment that she first admitted to herself that she was falling in love with Jean-Marc.

Isabel was in a quandary. There were only six days left before Jean-Marc was to return to France. She had heard that men could be slow to make declarations of love and something within her told her that she would have to speak first. There was no time to wait for him to arrive at the realization that he loved her.

She was certain he did love her. All of his endearments and solicitous behavior toward her told her that. She, in her turn, was dreaming of possible scenarios that would play out once he knew her true feelings. She would accompany him back to France. They could live together for a time that would, of course, simply be a prelude to the marriage that would inevitably follow. She would enroll at the Sorbonne and, once she had finished her education, she would have his babies - as many as he wanted - and she would delight in caring for him and for them. She would take pains to determine his preferences and would do everything in her power to give him a carefree, harmonious home. She trembled inwardly at the thought of his making love to her and she wanted nothing more than to surrender to a mutual passion, to meld with his body, to give him joy.

Now, without delay, she had to find an opportunity to tell him all of this. She would have to make an excuse to be alone with him in a place where she could be certain they would not be interrupted.

The next day was grey with a series of thunderstorms that did little to diminish the oppressive heat, but the following morning lived up to the forecast of beautiful weather. There was a high, with temperatures in the low eighties and a cloudless sky. As Isabel, Andrew, and Jean-Marc finished their afternoon's work, Jean-Marc asked if they would like to take a stroll down the street after dinner. He was particularly interested in the architecture of the adjacent mid-nineteenth century houses in the historic district and since, at twilight, people already had their lights on and their windows and doors open to catch the breeze, one could glimpse something of the interiors by walking past.

"I am," he said, chuckling, "what you call a peering Tom?"

"A peeping Tom," Andrew said.

"A voyeur?" Jean-Marc asked.

"That has more of a sexual connotation than I hope you mean in this particular instance," Andrew smiled. "If you were looking for nude people in their bedrooms, then 'voyeur' and 'peeping Tom' yes. But if you want to see from a distance how our neighbors have decorated their front halls and living rooms, that's mild curiosity, and it's not illegal."

"I have no intention of having a time with the police," Jean-Marc laughed.

"We call it having a 'run-in' with the police; it's a colloquialism," Isabel said. "And yes to your question. I will happily go for a walk with you."

"You have studied about architecture and the decoration of interiors?" Jean-Marc asked her.

"No, not really. But my grandmother and mother have always been very interested in such things, and some of that has rubbed off on me, I guess," Isabel replied.

"Well, you two have fun," Andrew said. "I've almost finished the mystery I'm reading, and, after dinner, I intend to find out 'who-done-it.'"

Isabel silently blessed him for the opportunity this afforded her.

That night at supper, Isabel's grandmother commented that she appeared flushed and was concerned at how little she was eating. "I do hope you are not catching a fever."

"No, no I'm fine, really - just not very hungry." Isabel said, wishing dinner to be over and listening for Jean-Marc's knock at the door. Finally it came and Isabel jumped to her feet, dropping her napkin on the floor. As she bent to retrieve it, she murmured, "That will be Jean-Marc. We are going for a walk," and she ran out the door.

They walked slowly together as people do who are

WHILE THE MUSIC LASTS

comfortable in each other's company. But Isabel's mind was racing, though she had barely spoken a word of greeting.

"Well," Jean-Marc sighed, "I will be in Paris at this time next week. This summer has gone too quickly."

"Yes," Isabel agreed.

"I like this town with its beautiful houses. Perhaps when you do your junior year program in Grenoble, you can stop in Paris first and let me show you the city."

Isabel was silent.

"You are quiet tonight." Jean-Marc said. "A penny for your thoughts... is that the expression?"

"Yes," Isabel replied and then realized that the moment had come. She would have to tell him what she felt.

"I don't want to wait until my junior year," she said. "I told you my parents and I are going to Italy, to Venice, next month."

Jean-Marc looked at her and nodded.

"Well, I want to stay on in Europe after that. I don't want to come back to the States. I want to go to Paris – to be there with you."

Jean-Marc stopped and turned to face her. He looked perplexed. Slapping at a mosquito on his arm, he asked, "But how would that be possible? You will start college in a very short time. It would be wrong to come to Paris when there is so little time."

"Oh, Jean-Marc, don't you see? What I am trying to say is that I love you. And, although you may not know it yet, you love me too. We are so good together! We are meant to be with each other. I can't let you go without me. I would miss you so terribly."

"I will miss you, too, Isabel. But you can't mean what you say – that you love me."

WHILE THE MUSIC LASTS

"Yes!" Isabel shook her head impatiently. "Please, you must understand. Someday, I want to be your wife!"

"My wife?" Jean-Marc repeated, "My wife?"

"Yes, yes, I want to take care of you and…"

Jean-Marc took his index finger and pressed firmly it against her lips. "Don't go on," he said. "This can never be."

"Why can't it be?" Isabel stammered. "All you have to do is agree!"

"That is something I cannot do. I cannot agree."

"But why? I…"

"Because, I am not ready to get married and…"

"We wouldn't need to be married right away! I…"

"No!" Jean–Marc interrupted. "There is a girl in France, the daughter of my parents' closest friends. It has always been assumed that we would marry one day. If I refused her the damage would be terrible – how do you say it – psycho… psychologically."

Isabel inhaled deeply to steady herself. At such a crucial time, how could he be worrying about semantics? "But do you love her?"

"In France, we do not necessarily see love and marriage in the same way you do here. I will marry her. Certainly, I will never marry you." Jean-Marc's eyes were cold and his expression took on a hardness Isabel had never seen before.

As the full impact of his words struck her, the blow made her chest ache.

When she was small, she had been in Central Park one day and some boys were playing with a baseball nearby. She had not seen the ball coming toward her and it had hit her full in the stomach, knocking the wind out of her. The woman in charge of the boys marched the guilty boy

WHILE THE MUSIC LASTS

over to apologize and Isabel forgave him immediately. It had obviously been an accident. But what Jean-Marc was saying was no accident.

She had not known such pain existed. Fortunately some instinct of self-preservation took hold of her. Her pride, it seemed, was not dead. She would not let him know what he was doing to her. She would never let anyone know what had happened on this particular evening.

Forcing herself to speak in a calm, low voice, she said, "Yes, I understand. If you really feel that way, then I have made a dreadful mistake."

She turned and made herself start to walk slowly back toward the house. Though all she wanted was to reach the privacy of her room, she would not let him see her run. Then she heard Jean-Marc say, "Wait!"

Suddenly, he took her by the hand and led her down an adjacent driveway into a grove of trees where it was very dark. Holding her by her shoulders, he pushed her against the trunk of a maple and, lifting her face, he kissed her hard on the mouth. Isabel, thoroughly confused, yielded to his kiss and felt herself melting into his embrace. She had probably misunderstood what he had just said, or he had spoken incorrectly, but none of that mattered now that his lips were on hers. But he continued kissing her so hard that her mouth was pressed sharply against her teeth and he was hurting her. Simultaneously, he thrust his hand down her blouse wrenching off its top button to grab her breast. Pulling her away from the tree, he forced her down until she was lying on her back on the ground. Reaching under her skirt, he tore her underpants and, jamming his knee against her thigh, he tried to force her legs apart. Everything he was doing was rough and hurried. His fingernails scratched her skin, and his breathing was short and deep. Isabel began to struggle against him saying, "No! No!"

He cupped a hand over her mouth, hissing, "Merde! Shut up!"

Things could not have gone more terribly wrong. This was not love. This had nothing to do with love. Isabel couldn't breathe, and she began to fight with all her strength, kicking and biting and crying until, finally, he stopped.

He gave a sarcastic laugh. "You are a little tigress, no?"

She was out of breath and sucking in air in great gulps. "Why?" she asked, sobbing. "You don't love me, so why?"

"I don't love you, but why should that stop us from having fun?"

Isabel could not believe what he was saying. She struggled to her feet and he reached for her again, pinching the flesh of her inner thigh. She kicked him in the groin and when he groaned, she began to run. She ran the two blocks back to her grandparents' front walk and, opening the little wrought-iron gate, hurried to the house. It was completely dark now. She hastily rearranged her clothing and ran her hand through her hair. All she wanted was to reach the safety of her room. She climbed the stairs, closed the door behind her and sat rocking backward and forward on the edge of her bed. She turned on her radio and muffled her sobs with pillows. She wanted her mother – oh, how she wanted her mother. She wished she were a baby again and could "go into the picture" in Venice, cradled in her mother's arms. Venice! Oh, God, they were to leave for Venice in less than two weeks. How could she travel feeling like this? She felt as battered and bloodied as a child who has fallen headlong on a gravel path. Her hand was on the telephone receiver but she could not raise it to dial her parents' number. They would be devastated if she told them that she had nearly been raped. "It is best to say nothing. I'm grown now. I must manage this on my own." Repeating this to herself over and over, she waited until it was very late, then crept downstairs and opened the liquor cabinet. She poured a stiff drink of whiskey and took it back to her room. She thought she wanted to get drunk. She knew she wanted oblivion, but she was not sure exactly how to get it. She hoped she had enough liquor to do the job properly. No sooner had she forced it down than she began to feel miserably nauseated. She ran to the bathroom and vomited.

Her grandmother heard her retching and knocked on the door.

"Isabel, darling, you are sick, aren't you?"

Isabel gasped for air. "Yes, Nana, I think I have a stomach flu."

"I'm so sorry. I thought you looked a little peculiar at dinner. Is there anything I can do for you - anything at all I can get for you?"

"No, thank you," Isabel said through the door. I think I'll be able to sleep now. After some good sleep, I'm sure I'll be fine."

Isabel pleaded illness during the few days until Jean-Marc's departure. Her grandmother carried trays to her room bringing her foods she felt would most benefit an invalid: weak tea and dry toast alternated with milk toast and tapioca pudding. Much of this Isabel took to the bathroom and flushed down the toilet. She could not bear to hurt her grandmother's feelings by overtly refusing the meals, but she had almost no appetite.

Her mind was reeling and her body ached from the physical struggle. Examining the bruises on her arms and legs, she wondered at her own naïveté. How she could have been such an incredibly bad judge of character?

Unable to sleep for more than a few hours each night, Isabel lay in the dark reliving what had happened. She had managed to escape with her virginity intact, but she knew that Jean-Marc had succeeded in raping her emotionally. A part of her was mourning the loss of a man she had loved and with whom she had thought she wanted to spend the rest of her life. It was galling to have to accept the bitter fact that this man had never existed except in her imagination.

Eventually, with Jean-Marc gone and her grandmother threatening to make a doctor's appointment for her, Isabel dressed in clothing that covered the remaining bruises, which had turned from a deep purple to a pale yellowish green, and came downstairs. Her grandparents were very concerned about her pallor and the dark circles under her eyes.

"My poor baby," her grandmother said. "You have been through a real siege, haven't you?"

Isabel smiled wanly. "Yes," she said, "but I'm beginning to feel better."

"About time, too," her grandfather said giving her a hug. "We've been worried about you."

Two days later, Isabel began packing. She would be returning to New York soon. She tried to rekindle her early enthusiasm about the trip to Italy, but the trauma she had recently endured left her with a pervasive indifference not only to Venice but to the world at large. She picked up her French books and threw them into her suitcase. She would try to do well on the language placement exams at Swarthmore but only because she wanted to take as few courses in French as possible - just enough, in fact, to satisfy her foreign language requirement. Majoring in French was no longer an option for her. She had no idea what subject would replace it.

Isabel was beginning to make up the sleep she had lost after Jean-Marc's brutality. One night her dreams were disturbed by the annoying, insistent ringing of a bell... the telephone? The bell stopped... a wrong number. Only half awake, Isabel sighed and turned over. But then, someone was crying. She sat up with a start and looked at the illuminated hands of her clock. It was three a.m. Down the hall, her grandmother was crying inconsolably. Isabel turned on her light, got up, opened her door and peered into the hall. The lamp next to the telephone on the lowboy was lit, dimly illuminating the far end of the corridor. This one small point of light in a long, high-ceilinged space made the darkness in the rest of the hall seem almost menacing. Isabel ran to her grandparents who were clinging to each other outside their bedroom door.

"What is it? What's wrong?"

Isabel's grandmother was crying too hard to answer her. But her grandfather reached out his hand and clasped her to him.

"It's your mother," he said. "She had a heart attack."

"But she'll be all right?" Isabel said. "She'll be all right, won't she?" she repeated emphatically.

"No, darling," her grandfather replied. "Oh, Isabel, sweetheart, she's dead."

From a great distance, Isabel heard something about plans to leave at daybreak. She went back to her room and quietly closed her door. When her grandparents came to get her two hours later, they found her sitting on her bed holding clumps of hair that she had pulled from her scalp. Blood was running down her face and dripping on her nightgown.

The Samuel Tuke Psychiatric Hospital, named after the late eighteenth-century Quaker who founded the first humane asylum for the mentally ill in York, England, was situated in the foothills of the Poconos about an hour's drive from the town where Isabel's grandparents lived. It had extensive grounds with beautifully manicured lawns, and as they drove through the gates, Isabel pretended that she was a weekend guest at some large estate. It was a very hot day with grey skies and high humidity.

The admitting room was small. The staff turned on the air conditioner and left Isabel alone so long that she began to shiver. When the social worker and the psychiatric nurse came, they had her sign a lot of forms. The admitting doctor asked her what the trouble was, and when she tried to tell him, he kept looking at his watch. Finally, he said, "It can't hurt you to stay here for awhile." And so she was admitted.

They took Isabel to a room on an open floor. She asked what the difference was between an open floor and a closed floor and was told that, on a closed floor, the door was kept locked at all times. She was to be given individual privileges that meant she had the freedom of the grounds. Group privileges meant someone always had to accompany you. And then there were people with no privileges at all. As she was entering her building, she noticed that some of the windows were barred. She was told that, whenever she left the hall for any reason, she had to sign out and sign in.

WHILE THE MUSIC LASTS

If she went to the cafeteria, she had to sign out; the same would be true if she went for a walk.

The patients' rooms were so small that they reminded Isabel of prison cells she had seen in films, and they all had doors with little windows with tiny curtains strung over them on the outside. Apparently, here, privacy was a privilege as well. Her room was hot and stifling, so they unlocked the screen to turn on her air conditioner. When she asked if she could regulate the air conditioner herself they told her no. Someone would always have to come to unlock the screen. Then they went through her luggage: her suitcase, her carry-on bag, and her purse. They took away her aspirin, her throat lozenges, her vitamin pills, her laxative, her skin lotion, her scissors, her sewing kit, her tweezers and her razor.

She panicked then and wanted to leave and cried out, "I'm not insane!"

Two nurses came and sat with her and told her they knew it was frightening at first, but she would get used to it.

"See how upset you are? You need to be here."

"Think of it as though you were being treated for a broken leg. It's just an illness of another part of the body."

But they didn't understand. She didn't have a broken leg; she had a broken heart, and she couldn't equate the two then or ever.

Soon a succession of people came with pads and pens and asked her questions and made notations. The questions all seemed the same and all ran into one another. She remembered a time when she had been mugged and had had to go to a police station to make a report, and there they had made her tell the same story to five different

WHILE THE MUSIC LASTS

people. She decided this was a similar procedure.

How was she feeling?

Depressed.

Why was she there?

Because she had loved a man who didn't love her and because her mother, who had loved her - who had been devoted to her, was dead. She could not bring herself to divulge the details of Jean-Marc's attempted rape. She knew that the attack had not been her fault, but she felt a deep and irrational sense of shame.

Did she want to kill herself?

No, she had other people who cared for her - her father and her grandparents, and she couldn't do that to them. Beyond that she wouldn't much care if she lived or died.

If she thought of suicide, how would she do it?

This startled her. She tried to think of ways people killed themselves. She remembered hearing her parents discussing people in the Bloomsbury group. They had talked of how Virginia Woolf had drowned herself and of how Dora Carrington had been deeply in love with Lytton Strachey although he was homosexual. After he died, she felt she couldn't go on, and she shot herself. But Isabel really couldn't see drowning or shooting herself. She told them she thought she might just swallow some pills.

"Where would you get the pills?"

Isabel didn't know and didn't want to think about it, so she told them the first answer that came into her head: "I would look in the medicine cabinet."

They wrote down every word she said.

A nurse, plump and about fifty with short greying hair and a pleasant smile, took her temperature and blood pressure. Isabel told her that she had not been able to sleep since her mother died. The nurse patted her on the shoulder and said she would mention this to the doctor.

At nine in the evening Isabel went to the women's room to shower. There were three stalls. A woman was using one shower and had her nightclothes on a chair in front of it. Isabel asked if she could share the back of her chair.

"Sure," she said, "I'm finished." Her face was red and her eyes were puffy as though she had been crying.

Isabel came out of the shower and brushed her teeth, and when she looked up, a thin young girl with long, flowing yellow hair and violet eyes was standing beside her.

"Hi," she said quietly, "I'm Joan."

"Hi, I'm Isabel."

"How are you feeling?"

"A little scared."

"You'll be okay - it's the best place around. This your first time in?"

Isabel nodded. "Yours?"

"No, my second. Good luck," she said and offered her hand.

"I'm sorry," Isabel said. "My hands are wet."

"That doesn't matter." She took Isabel's wet hand in hers and then left as quietly as she had come in.

Isabel went to bed at ten and lay staring at the ceiling until nearly eleven when she fell into a light sleep. She woke abruptly at twelve when she heard her door closing. She started crying softly into her pillow. Oh, Mother, she thought, I need you so right now. Jean-Marc, why couldn't you be the man I wanted you to be? I have so much to give and it's all such a waste - such a damned waste.

At one a.m. she went out and spoke to the night nurse.

"I was asleep, but I heard someone come into my room and close my door when they left. They woke me, and now I can't get back to sleep."

WHILE THE MUSIC LASTS

The nurse had a pronounced Irish accent and she explained gently that they had to make rounds every hour to check on the patients.

"But I will leave your door ajar a bit. That way you won't be disturbed again. Let me just check your chart." She went through some papers. "Yes, the doctor has prescribed a Diazepam, if necessary. That will help you to sleep."

The pill worked after about forty minutes, and Isabel slept from two until six thirty. They would not allow her to eat breakfast because they had to do blood tests first. The technician came and put a rubber strap around her arm and drew out three large vials of blood. Isabel thought, "If I had cut my wrists, that color would have run out all over everything."

By then it was too late to go to the cafeteria, so she was told to eat a snack in the kitchen on her hall. Three other patients were sitting around the table.

"You aren't a patient, are you?" they asked. "You seem so cool and collected."

Isabel wanted to explain that she normally presented a calm exterior to the world no matter how much she was seething inside. But she didn't say that; she just told them, "Yes, I'm a patient."

Isabel went searching through the cupboards and finally found some Bran Flakes. There were large paper cups and spoons set out on one of the counters. She asked where the cereal bowls were. A middle-aged, rotund man with long sparse sandy hair combed over his bald spot, identified himself as Rick and said, "Use the paper cups, they're bigger. The cereal bowls are so small, they don't hold anything."

So Isabel poured the cereal into a cup and filled two

other cups with milk and juice and sat down.

Rick joked with her, "One thing you gotta be to sit here - one thing you gotta be to join this club: we're all crazy." Then he became serious. "You know what my psychiatrist asked me? He asked me if I'd mind if he wrote down that I was paranoid, insane. He asked if I'd mind!"

Josephine, an elderly woman of about seventy with long, white hair twisted into a bun, told Isabel she had been a social worker.

"One day they found me walking down the middle of the street in my nightgown," she said.

Rick repeated, "We're all crazy here."

Isabel said, "I don't remember who, but someone once maintained that madness is a sane reaction to the way the world treats you."

Everyone nodded and agreed.

Suddenly, Isabel felt tears welling up in her eyes. She looked down at her soggy Bran Flakes floating in a paper cup and thought, "My God, it's come to this. It's really come to this."

Josephine touched her arm. "You're very pretty," she said.

After breakfast a nurse came to take Isabel over to another building for a chest x-ray.

"Put your arms over your head and hold your breath."

Next she was taken to a room with an examining table with a long strip of clean paper running down the middle of it. The technician told her to take everything off except her underpants, put on a robe, tie it in the front and lie down.

A young girl with blonde hair came in to do an EKG. She apologized: she said she knew it could be a bit embarrassing. She had to put sticky things in various places around Isabel's left breast to attach the recording instrument. Isabel told her not to worry, that physical exams didn't bother her.

The girl said, "Well, you never know what to expect from patients. When I was a new technician on one of my first cases, I came into a room and said, "Okay, Mr. Jones, are you ready? He took off his robe and said, 'I'm ready whenever you are.'" She laughed and said, "I told him I didn't think I was ready for that! He said it was too bad because he'd always liked blondes."

While the girl was attaching the EKG monitor to her breast, Isabel had a sudden flashback to the attack. She was there again. She could feel Jean-Marc's hand touching her. She could hear him breathing. Without meaning to, she suddenly stiffened.

The technician was concerned. "Are you still okay?"

"Yes, I'm sorry. It's just that a man attacked me and he grabbed my breast."

This was the first time she had told anyone.

"Oh, no! He didn't rape you did he?" The girl looked at Isabel. Was this something she needed to report?

"No, I fought him off. Don't worry. I'm okay."

Soon after the technician left, a doctor came in. He was very solemn. "Breathe in; breathe out. Say ahh. Walk in a straight line."

Then it was time for lunch. The nurse who had brought Isabel over could not leave because she had to fill out some papers. Another nurse told her, "It's okay. She can go by herself. She's on individual privileges." But the first nurse seemed uncertain. "I don't want to do that. I wasn't told to do that."

The second nurse persisted, "It's all right because she's on individual."

WHILE THE MUSIC LASTS

And so it was decided that Isabel could go to lunch.

Although it took her a long time to admit it to herself, Isabel eventually found some comfort in all of the rules and the strict regimentation. She did what she was told. There was no need to think beyond that.

The cafeteria was crowded and noisy and bare in the way institutional rooms are bare: no carpets, no curtains - just linoleum and plastic tables with plastic chairs.

Isabel was not very hungry. She took a roll, some vegetable soup, a glass of water and an orange drink. She didn't know anyone, so she went to a table and sat alone. She could overhear snatches of conversations:

"It won't do any good if he won't talk to the psychiatrist. Today they both just sat and looked out of the window."

"Frances is scheduled for her first shock treatment on Monday."

Isabel ate the roll dry with no butter and looked at the corn and lima beans floating in the soup. She drank the tangy, sparkling orangeade for dessert and was about to pick up her tray to return it when she saw Joan, the blonde girl who had spoken to her in the shower room the night before, approaching her. Joan stood awkwardly at the end of the table. "Would it be okay if I sit with you; I mean, would you mind?"

Isabel felt too exhausted to be sociable, but the girl had a pathetic demeanor, and Isabel did not have the heart to say no.

Joan sat beside her and the two were silent for several moments. In an attempt to be friendly, Isabel said, "You told me this was your second time here?"

Joan stared at her food, and Isabel was afraid her question could be seen as prying. She was about to apologize when Joan sighed and said softly, "I was here for the first time five years ago. I didn't know what was wrong with me. The world around me all seemed strange as if I were looking at it through a glass that was distorting everything. I couldn't shake the feeling, and I got really scared."

Isabel said, "That must have been awful."

Joan answered, "After some intense therapy, I got better. They said it was something called neurasthenia, but I found out later that they thought I might be schizophrenic." She was silent again, and Isabel was uncertain how to respond. She decided to wait to see if Joan wanted to say more. Joan clasped her arms tightly together in front of her and continued. "There's no secret about why I'm in here now. I'm here because my brother just killed himself, and I'm the only one who knows it – except for the psychiatrist, I mean. My parents would never be able to understand it, so he left a note for me where he knew only I would find it."

Isabel put her hand on Joan's shoulder, but Joan didn't seem to notice. "We're Catholics, you see, and my mother always hoped my brother would become a priest. He was drawn to the church, but in the end it failed him. He studied for the priesthood because he knew he would never marry. He was gay. He told me once that he could not understand why God made people 'queer' and then damned them if they acted on it. The priesthood offered a life of celibacy and he took it. But you shouldn't become a priest to escape from something. You should only become a priest if you feel an overwhelming calling. He learned this too late, and, eventually, he started drinking too much. Last month he overdosed on alcohol and sleeping pills. The doctor was nice and told my parents it was a mistake. He said my brother made a mistake – that it was an accident. But the note he left me said 'I don't want to go on. I'm drinking this bourbon and taking these pills – whether in sufficient dosage, I don't know. If they kill me, I'm guilty of suicide. I'm probably damned. Pray for me if you think prayer matters. I don't know anymore.'"

Isabel gave Joan a spontaneous hug. For the first time since her mother died, she was able to grasp that she was not alone in having problems and to feel sympathy for someone else's pain.

When Isabel went back to her room to rest, two women, both in their thirties, she thought, were waiting to talk with her. One was very thin with an angular jaw and stringy brown hair; the other wore heavy black-rimmed glasses and no make-up, not even lipstick. They explained that they were occupational therapists, and they asked her to sew together pieces of leather using increasingly difficult stitches. They watched what she did and wrote down how well she did it. They told her she could go to work in the craft room or play some games in musical therapy.

Isabel felt anger then. She wished she could take their pieces of leather and throw them across the room. But she said simply, "You know, I'm really tired. What I'd like to do is just take a nap."

The women looked at each other, nodded and left.

Isabel lay down and was beginning to doze when some workmen put a ladder against her window and climbed to the roof over her head and started hammering and dropping things and shouting and whistling. They were repairing something directly above her. She wanted to scream. She wanted to bang against the walls and tell them to leave her alone. She wanted the world and everything and everyone in it just to leave her alone. But she did not make a sound. She clenched her fists and curled up in the fetal position and wished herself dead.

Stepping into Dr. Rebecca Roth's office was like walking into an oasis. Leaving behind the bright fluorescent lights and the plastic, metal and linoleum surfaces of the rest of the hospital – surfaces that seemed to amplify every sound, Isabel first noticed the pleasant indirect lighting and the silence. The hunter green carpet was soft beneath her feet, and the furniture, a small sofa and two chairs, was upholstered in a welcoming muted plaid that picked up the colors of the carpet and the paler green walls. Isabel was relieved to see that there was no chaise longue or anything resembling a Freudian couch.

The doctor, seated behind a pale oak desk, rose, smiled and shook hands. She motioned Isabel to a chair opposite her. Rebecca Roth was about forty, Isabel guessed, and had lustrous, black curly hair that set off her pale skin and large, kindly brown eyes.

Isabel glanced at the shelves behind the doctor that were full of books, three conch shells, a copy of a Chagall print in a silver frame, and a small menorah.

Dr. Roth shifted in her chair and folded her hands together on her desk. "You have some issues that are bothering you?"

Isabel nodded.

"Would you like to talk about them?"

Isabel, uncertain where to begin, blurted out, "I was in love with a boy who told me he didn't love me. Right after that my mother died suddenly. She had a heart attack. Before that, nobody knew there was anything wrong with her heart."

"So you were totally unprepared for her loss?"

"Yes."

"You and your mother were very close?"

"Yes, very." Isabel's lower lip began to quiver.

"And the boy? What can you tell me about him? How long had you known him?"

"He was from France. He came to America over the summer to improve his English. I knew him for about two months."

"During that time you developed feelings for him, feelings that you thought he might reciprocate?"

"Yes, at first, he was really nice to me. But when I told him I loved him, he was horrible."

"Horrible?"

Tears welled up in Isabel's eyes and she took a tissue from the box beside her chair.

"Take your time."

"He… he told me he was going to marry a French girl and then everything went wrong."

"How did things go wrong?"

"He said he didn't love me but that we could 'have fun.'"

"Fun?"

"He tried to force himself on me. I kicked him hard and I got away. But now I have awful nightmares – about the attack and about my mother. The dreams are all jumbled up, and I wake up with a start and I'm terrified. Then I can't get back to sleep. Sometimes I don't sleep more than four hours. I'm just exhausted, but I can't sleep."

"Perhaps that's where we should begin. There are several things we can try to help you sleep."

"There are?"

"Yes, I'm going to start you on a nightly regimen of a low dose of Diazepam. This is not a long-term solution, but it usually works well at first. Then I can teach you relaxation techniques. We might even get into some biofeedback and self-hypnosis. I just want you to know that there are several possible solutions."

"I've been thinking that I'd never be able to sleep well anymore."

"That's the sort of thinking that we are going to work to change. I'm going to help you. We'll work things through together."

Isabel left her first session with Dr. Roth feeling hopeful. She liked her psychiatrist, and she was glad she was a woman. It would be easier to confide in a woman.

A month into her hospitalization, Andrew came to visit. Isabel saw him in the waiting room before he saw her. He was sitting hunched over with his hands in his lap. When he saw her approaching, he stood and came toward her. This was not the Andrew Isabel had always known. His usual happy demeanor was gone. This Andrew was sober and quiet. He hugged her to him, then took her by the shoulders and stared into her eyes.

"Oh, Isabel," he said.

"Andrew," Isabel replied and, keeping her voice light, said, "how wonderful of you to come! I'm so happy to see you."

"I'm so sorry about everything - so terribly sorry."

Isabel was not sure how she should respond, so she said simply, "Thank you."

"How are they treating you in this place?"

"Well, it's not exactly the Ritz -" Isabel was trying desperately to achieve some of the usual levity between them, "but according to those in the know, I'm making good progress."

"I feel so awful, it was…"

Isabel did not want to relive the trauma of her mother's sudden death, so she decided to speak about it first and then quickly try to change the subject.

"Losing mother was a dreadful shock, of course, but my therapist is being very good in helping me to deal with it."

"But I feel so guilty. A lot of this is my fault."

"Your fault?" Isabel said incredulously. "How can you possibly think that?"

"I was the one who introduced you to Jean-Marc. I was the one who was so eager to have you meet him."

Isabel could not believe what Andrew was saying. "You mean," she said, " he told you about…"

"Yes, he told me you were in love with him. I told him he was a damned lucky fellow. But then he said he had turned you away. I felt like giving him a good bash on the nose, let me tell you." Andrew paused and then said, "He isn't worth it, Isabel. I know. Remember the day we celebrated his birthday? That afternoon, about four o'clock, he got a call from his parents in France, and he took it in the study. I was reading on my bed, and my bedroom is just above the study. The windows were open and I wasn't trying to listen, but I couldn't help hearing some of the conversation because Jean-Marc was speaking loudly and laughing. Of course, he was speaking rapidly in French and probably thought no one was near enough to be able to understand, but I got the gist of what he was saying. He was being snide about America and about Americans in general. He kept making disparaging remarks."

Isabel stared wide-eyed at Andrew.

"It's true," Andrew said emphatically. "You know I

would never lie to you."

"I know." Isabel hesitated. Finally she said, "It wasn't just that he turned me away. It was worse than that - worse than you know."

"Worse?"

"Yes, Jean-Marc tried to rape me."

"My God, the bastard! Why didn't you call the police?"

"Because he didn't succeed. I managed to get away."

"My God," Andrew repeated. "Oh, Isabel!"

Andrew looked so dejected that all Isabel could think of was comforting him. She took his hands and smiled at him and said, "I shouldn't have told you. But, please, none of this is in any way your fault. And, besides, I'm getting better. Truly, I am."

It was only later that Isabel realized she was angry but not surprised that Jean-Marc had talked of her to Andrew.

When she told Dr. Roth what Andrew had said about Jean-Marc, Dr. Roth asked how it made her feel.

"I feel furious at him. His telling Andrew was just a betrayal."

"And...?" Dr. Roth said gently, encouraging her to elaborate.

"Well, I've been thinking about men in general, and I doubt that I'll ever be able to love anyone as freely as I loved Jean-Marc. I mean, my mother once gave me some of Elizabeth Barrett Browning's and Robert Browning's love letters to read and I was impressed by how tender and passionate they were. But I'm scared of that kind of all-consuming love. That sort of love was partly responsible for putting me in here."

"But surely there are loves you know about, personally, that have been beneficial instead of harmful?"

WHILE THE MUSIC LASTS

Isabel hesitated. "Yes," she said finally. "The love my parents had, and the love my grandparents still have."

"I thought so," Dr. Roth replied.

"But," Isabel went on, "I'd be very, very careful next time. One of the main things I've developed in my therapy with you is a strong sense of survival."

Dr. Roth smiled.

———

A large snowstorm blanketed the area in mid-December. Isabel had been hospitalized for three and one half months, and she was waiting for her session with Dr. Roth who was, uncharacteristically, late. Finally the doctor appeared, shaking snow off of the hood of her heavy, wool coat and carrying her shoes in her hand. She asked Isabel to come into the office and proceeded to take off her sturdy boots, stowing them in the corner. While putting on her shoes, she said, "Forgive me for keeping you waiting. There was a traffic accident, just a fender bender because of all the snow – but cars were backed up for blocks. I had the radio on and the announcer said there were delays of up to an hour. I nearly decided to go home and call in to reschedule. But, I particularly wanted to see you today."

"You did? Why?"

Dr. Roth smiled and said, "How would you feel about getting out of this place in time for Christmas?"

Isabel wasn't sure exactly how she felt. She was happy and frightened at the same time. It would be wonderful to be home with her dad for the holidays, but the thought of leaving the safety of the hospital environment scared her.

"It would be great to be home, but…"

"But you are feeling a little apprehensive as well?"

"I guess so."

"That's not unusual. But I'm really terribly pleased with your progress. You have confronted a lot of important issues and dealt with them. Do you know what the turning point was for me?"

Isabel shook her head.

"You started replacing the hurt you felt at the way Jean-Marc treated you with justifiable anger. That was real progress."

Isabel smiled. "I would love to go home, if you think I'm ready."

"Why don't we try you at home next weekend and see how it goes? Perhaps I'm putting the cart before the horse, but I really think it might be beneficial for you to think of starting college next semester."

"You mean in the middle of the year?"

"Why not?"

Isabel greeted this news with enthusiasm. "Oh, that would be fantastic!"

"Remember I'd be just a phone call or a train ride away. And I can give you a prescription for Diazepam if you need it to sleep while you're getting settled in. Once you adjust to the new routine, I think you'll be fine."

Isabel knew this was the best Christmas present she could have asked for.

PART THREE

What might have been and what has been
Point to one end, which is always present.
Footfalls echo in the memory
Down the passage which we did not take
Towards the door we never opened
Into the rose garden.

> T.S. Eliot
> Burnt Norton
> *Four Quartets*

WHILE THE MUSIC LASTS

    Isabel did well at college. She performed so ably on the French placement examinations that no further courses were necessary; she satisfied the language requirement. Her normal routine was rigorous, and her professors were demanding, but their teaching was generally excellent. She particularly enjoyed her classes in English literature and music. Throwing herself into her work, she thrived.

    Since she'd begun college at the second semester, she took several courses the next summer at the University of Pennsylvania. She wanted to catch up to her class and be able to graduate with them.

    Her first two years, Isabel roomed with girls who were friendly and compatible. Then, at a party at the end of her sophomore year, she met Alice Larsson, and the two of them got on famously from the start. Alice, a highly intelligent blonde, whose coloring made plain her Swedish heritage, had the sort of outgoing personality that complimented Isabel's more reserved demeanor. One could hardly be depressed around Alice's optimism. If Isabel saw the proverbial glass half empty, Alice saw one half full. After they had known each other a few weeks, Alice suggested that they walk over to the Scott amphitheater. It was the first warm day in May and the campus had been awash in colorful blooms since early spring. Beyond the row of faculty houses on Whittier Place, varieties of lilac lined the path to the Quaker meeting house. On Chester Road, across from the Episcopal church, magnolias in full splendor served as a background for wedding photographs, and the rose garden in the circle by McCabe library was showing early promise of the flowers to come. The open-air amphitheater in the woods, where graduation would soon be held, was silent except for the sounds of birdcalls and squirrels rustling in the nearby foliage. As they sat on the stone seats, Alice remarked, "You know I have roomed with Janet Alsop for two years?"

Isabel nodded.

"She's transferring to Barnard next fall. Her boyfriend goes to Columbia, and, I gather, it's getting serious between them."

"Oh," Isabel replied, hoping that Alice might be leading up to what she did, in fact, say next.

"If you don't have anyone definite lined up for the fall, I was wondering if you might like to room with me? I should warn you that people think I'm overly enthusiastic sometimes, but I don't snore and I keep my side of the room relatively neat. So…"

"I'd love to," Isabel broke in.

"To room with me?" Alice smiled, "Really?"

"Yes," Isabel answered emphatically.

They sat back and watched the dappled pattern the sun left on the ground as it shone through the new leaves. Isabel was delighted that Alice liked her enough to suggest that they room together.

Isabel dated sporadically but kept any relationship from turning serious. At the first sign that a boy wanted more than casual friendship, she immediately stopped seeing him. One evening, after breaking up with the third boy she had dated since knowing Alice, her friend, with her usual keen discernment, commented, "You won't let anyone of the opposite sex get too close, will you?"

"No, you're right; I won't," Isabel replied.

"Not that it's any of my business, but is there a reason? You can tell me to go jump in the lake if you like. I won't be offended."

"I don't mind sharing the reason with you. It's just that

WHILE THE MUSIC LASTS

I once had a very unhappy romance. Well, not a romance exactly. I desperately loved someone who didn't love me. He hurt me both emotionally and physically. After he told me that he didn't love me, he tried to force himself on me. It was a very ugly scene. Right after that happened, my mother died suddenly, and I guess you could say I had a breakdown. I still get prescriptions for a tranquilizer sometimes if I have trouble sleeping. But I rarely need to take one. In my case, I think the college doctor is overly concerned about my ability to handle stress. I honestly think he hasn't a clue how contented I am when I'm made to work hard intellectually."

"I knew about the pills. I went to borrow a pencil, once, and saw the bottle on your desk. I wasn't trying to pry, and I didn't say anything about it because I figured, if you wanted to talk about it, well, you would sometime."

"So now you know my darkest secrets," Isabel laughed.

"I may know some secrets but I don't understand why, just because you were hurt once, you won't give someone new a chance."

"I'm really scared - terrified actually. I admit it."

"Possibly you simply haven't met the right man yet."

"Possibly," Isabel sighed, and they left it there, although Alice made a mental note to introduce Isabel to her older brother, George. She and her brother were very close and she was certain that he and Isabel would like each other. She was also very aware of her brother's tenacity. When George put the full force of his personality behind something he wanted, he usually achieved the desired end.

WHILE THE MUSIC LASTS

George Larsson had left Yale to spend his junior year abroad at Pembroke College, Oxford. He took several tutorials with the college rector and the two became good friends.

George's father was a Missouri Synod Lutheran. George, raised in this church, accepted its rigid fundamentalist creed unquestioningly until he reached college and studied David Hume and the twentieth-century English logical positivists. It was then that he experienced a crisis of faith. By the end of the term, he still considered himself a theist but no longer a practicing Christian. He had no use for ethics based on the fear of punishment. He even questioned the atonement and justification by faith. How, he wondered, could a man who lived and died two thousand years ago possibly be relevant today?

George's loss of faith in Christianity left him feeling perplexed and incomplete. He was, by nature, gregarious and he found that he missed the sense of community and fellowship he had shared as a member of a congregation.

George's mother was a practicing Episcopalian. When he was young, his father would occasionally allow him to accompany her to Sunday services and George quite liked the liturgy, music, and ceremony of the high church. At Pembroke, he often found himself drawn to the chapel. It was a good place to sit quietly and think. Part of him wanted to replace Lutheran fundamentalism with his mother's less narrow faith. But he knew he would be deluding himself. The central problem of the divinity of Christ remained.

One morning, as they were walking out of chapel, George confided his struggle to the rector who stopped and suggested that they sit in one of the pews.

"I'm sure you know that you're not alone in experiencing this predicament," he said. "Many people before you have questioned their faith. In fact, I suspect that all of us have known doubt at one time or another. Even I, on occasion, waver and look for affirmation."

"What I need to know is how to get beyond the doubts and resolve the questions. How do I do that? How have other people gone about it?"

"There are various ways…" The rector paused before asking, "Did you read J. R. R. Tolkien's *Lord of the Rings* when you were a boy?"

"Yes! I loved his books."

"He invented his own mythology."

"Exactly, yes."

"And you felt caught up in and moved by his mythology?"

"Absolutely."

"Well," the rector went on, "Tolkien was a committed Christian. He said 'the story of Christ is simply a true myth'."

"I'm not sure I understand what that means."

"Tolkien argued that 'the doctrines which are extracted from the myth are less true then the myth itself.'"

"Less true…? I'm sorry," George said. "I'm afraid you've lost me."

"How can I put this?" the rector asked, rubbing his forehead. "Tolkien thought that ultimate truth is too vast and too important for the finite mind to be able to grasp it. That is why God needed to reveal Himself in a story we can understand… the story of Jesus."

George was silent. At length he said, "You're saying that God needed to clarify the truth for us, and even if we question some of the doctrines, the truth behind them is what really matters?"

"Precisely."

"I think I understand what you mean, but I'll need some time to consider it."

"Of course you will," the rector replied, smiling.

George began reading the poetry of Gerard Manley Hopkins. He made frequent visits to the chapel when he thought it most likely that he would be the only person there. He never knew how the combination of books, conversations with the rector, Tolkien's ideas and the Tudor Gothic architecture of the chapel achieved their purpose, but one day he experienced a sense of release and his doubts fell away. In accepting Christ, he felt in one sense humbled and, at the same time, somehow ennobled. As he focused very seriously on his new relationship with God, he began to wonder if, perhaps, he had a vocation to the Episcopal ministry.

By the time he returned to the United States, his mind was set on divinity school in New Haven. As he began his graduate studies, his professors, recognizing his ability in New Testament Greek, Latin and Hebrew, encouraged him to earn a doctorate and teach at the college level. But George, although he felt quite at home in the rarified atmosphere of an ivory tower, wanted to immerse himself in the more mundane aspects of a parish. He enjoyed baptisms and weddings, and he was pleased to offer what comfort he could at funerals.

He worked hard on his sermons to be sure that they were logical and coherent. When, as was often the case, they contained literary allusions, these were used solely to clarify by example and were never meant to bring merit to himself. He never belabored points, was not in the least interested in church politics, and had no ambition to rise in the church hierarchy.

George found his first charge, as assistant pastor in a

little church in a small town in Connecticut, much to his liking. There he was appreciated for the good, steady man that he was. The congregation found him trustworthy and saw him, at times, exhibit dogged perseverance when he believed a cause was right. They felt he was one of them, and that carried far more weight than any pulpit-pounding enthusiasm might have done. He emphasized the importance of a spirit of Christian community in the church and, although he wore Episcopal vestments, he would cite the Amish practice of coming together for a barn raising as a secular analogy of how his parishioners should work together for holy purposes.

Without mentioning it to anyone, he was looking for a wife: someone who could, quite literally, be a helpmate at home and in the church. Several eligible women he met he found too frivolous. He needed someone who thought as he did, who had staying power and seriousness of purpose. He prayed and trusted that he would meet her when the time was right.

All Isabel had felt, when she first arrived in Venice, was exhaustion. She did not care that her large, beautifully appointed room had a splendid view of the Grand Canal. She took her travel alarm clock from her carry-on bag and set it for two that afternoon, so she could shower, change her clothes and take a boat ride around the city before having dinner in the hotel dining room. As she lay back on the bed and closed her eyes, she began to make a mental note of what she most wanted to see. Along with all of the usual tourist highlights, she knew she did not want to miss the famed La Fenice, the opera house that burned in

1996 and had just recently reopened to the public. Isabel had read the story of the San Bernadetto Theater that had burned to the ground in 1774. When a new opera house was built in 1792, it was named La Fenice (the Phoenix) after the mythical bird that rose from the ashes of its dead parent. Isabel thought the name was either prescient or, if one were of a superstitious nature, ill-advised: not unlike calling the Titanic "unsinkable." The building burned again in 1836, rose once more in 1837, and was now in the process of its third incarnation.

As her alarm jarred her awake, Isabel was in no hurry to get up. She yawned, and stretched and thought, "Here I am, at last, in this most romantic of cities, the Venice of Robert Browning and Henry James, of Tiepolo and Titian." She rummaged through her bag and found her map. There was a vaporetto stop very close to the hotel.

It was late summer and the afternoon was sunny, although the air was brisk. Isabel sat by a window as the boat moved down the Canal, pulling into various landing stages. She watched as people boarded and disembarked and noticed the skill of the boatmen who were responsible for the safety of the passengers. The vaporetto was full but she knew that she had missed the larger crowds of a few weeks before when hordes of tourists had descended on the city.

She was entranced as the boat glided past the thirteenth-century "scuole" or guilds, churches and campaniles, palazzos, houses and clock towers. There was an incomparably rich variety of architectural styles. She saw carved Gothic cornerstones and Venetian Byzantine windows and, now and again, forms which showed clearly the influence of Northern Italian Renaissance sophistication. The city more than met all of her hopes.

WHILE THE MUSIC LASTS

Tomorrow morning she would visit the Basilica of St. Marks and the Doges Palace. Then, in the afternoon, if she were not too tired, she would take a vaporetto to the large, ornate palace of the Ca' Rezzonico, where Robert Browning died in 1889.

Isabel walked back to the Gritti Palace from the landing at Santa Maria del Giglio and enjoyed her meal of bigoli in salsa and fegato alla Veneziana, presented in quiet and elegant surroundings by perfectly trained and unobtrusive waiters.

Before her junior year, Isabel had to declare a major and gain acceptance in the department of her choice. The decision between music and English literature was a difficult one.

Intellectually and emotionally, Isabel was inspired by the genius of Bach. She enjoyed the challenge of playing the sonatas and working on the *Goldberg Variations: The Well Tempered Clavier.* She began studying the organ pieces and became proficient in some of the toccatas and fugues. Her taste was not limited to eighteenth-century music, for she loved most of the works she studied and heard, from chamber music through the lush, romantic concertos of Chopin, Tchaikovsky and Rachmaninoff. She was particularly fond of the dreamlike melodies of Debussy which, she was interested to learn, had been influenced by Impressionist paintings and poetry. In an art course she discovered that in the 1850s, before Debussy was even born, the artist Gustave Courbet, tired of seeing portraits that served primarily to flatter the wealthy, had introduced Realism. Impressionism followed with such

WHILE THE MUSIC LASTS

painters as Monet, Degas and Manet. While they went about revolutionizing ideas of perspective, form and light, Debussy similarly wanted to free music from "the barren traditions that stifled it." He wrote that his piano music was often meant "as a conversation between the piano and oneself."

Isabel also discovered poetry in college. Until then she had never shared her grandmother or mother's interest in the subject. In preparatory school she learned a few rather hackneyed verses that had meant nothing to her; but in one of her first college English classes she was introduced to the work of Emily Dickinson and knew almost immediately that, in this nineteenth-century, reclusive New England spinster, she had found a kindred spirit. Never before had Isabel read anyone who, often in simple quatrains, could express longing and anguish so profoundly. She committed to memory such lines as:

So We must meet apart -
You there – I – here -
With just the Door ajar
That Oceans are - and Prayer -
And that White Sustenance -
Despair -

After her first summer session at the University of Pennsylvania, Isabel asked her father to drive her to Amherst, Massachusetts, to visit the Dickinson house. Admission was by appointment only, so they had called ahead. A docent met them at the door, took them first into what had been the family parlor and then upstairs to the front, corner room that had been Emily Dickinson's domain. It was a lovely, simple room containing the poet's bed and desk and a few other necessary furnishings. Hanging on the closet door was one of Dickinson's white dresses.

Later that afternoon, Isabel went to a florist in town and purchased a single white rose that she took to the cemetery. The Dickinson plot was surrounded by a small wrought-iron fence. Isabel opened the little gate and placed the rose on the poet's grave.

After discovering Dickinson, Isabel read voraciously, beginning to appreciate Shakespeare for the first time, as well as poets as diverse as Christina Rossetti, T. S. Eliot, e.e. cummings and Rainer Maria Rilke. Studying the last, she wished she knew German, so she could read him in the original language, suspecting that, even in the best translation, something was lost.

The ambivalence in Isabel's mind about choosing a major was not easy to resolve. All through high school, music had been an extracurricular activity. She had, before Jean-Marc, seen French as her best subject. Was she attempting to replace French with another language – English? She knew this was unlikely because she saw the two very differently, and English was her native tongue. Looking at the problem from another viewpoint, she asked herself what she would do with her degree after graduation. Teaching was foremost in her thoughts. As much as she enjoyed literature, she knew she had little or no talent as a writer, and doubted that she possessed the ability of her favorite professors to make books come alive in a classroom. She understood that it would be folly to hope to make her living by playing the piano. Late nights in piano bars playing for patrons who were more interested in their drinks and conversation than in any selections she might choose held no appeal. However, with music, she could play for her own enjoyment, and then there was the definite possibility of a hands-on approach if she taught piano to young children. Isabel believed this would be preferable to trying to introduce bored adolescents to Shakespeare. Music slowly gained the ascendancy and, ultimately, she chose it as her major.

Isabel found that she could lose herself while working at the piano. During practice sessions, the hours raced by and, often, feeling she had barely begun, she had to stop. She decided to try for honors in piano after winning the Fennimore music award for outstanding pianist, which paid for her private lessons. Taking honors meant that she would have to perform a senior honors recital that would be more rigorous than the recital required of all majors. They simply had to demonstrate proficiency on a keyboard instrument by playing a two-part invention of J.S. Bach and the first movement of an easy late eighteenth or early nineteenth-century sonata.

She was not entirely undaunted by the prospect of trying for honors, but her trepidation served as a healthy stimulus to work even harder. She realized that majoring in music did not mean she had to abandon English literature. She would take enough credits to satisfy the requirements for a minor in the English department.

By the end of their senior year with honors examinations just a few weeks ahead, Isabel and Alice found that they had little time to sleep. Alice was taking honors in psychology. She and Isabel were experiencing the heady atmosphere of those who are about to graduate. They could not yet take pride in their accomplishments, but that goal was within reach.

There was a nascent sadness that they would no longer be roommates and that this phase of their lives was ending. But such nostalgia was pushed aside as they concentrated all of their efforts on doing well for the examiners who were brought in from other colleges and universities. These strangers would determine whether they received honors, high honors, highest honors or, rarely, in some instances, no honors at all.

Plans were being made to invite parents and relatives to graduation. Rooms in Ashton House on campus and motel rooms off campus were at a premium. Alice and Isabel had booked well in advance, so that Alice's parents and brother and Isabel's father and grandparents would be staying within a short distance of the campus. During graduation week, the relatives planned sightseeing trips to Philadelphia and Pennsylvania Dutch country in Lancaster County.

Alice was full of anticipation as the moment neared to introduce Isabel to her brother. Isabel had auditioned for and won the right to play a solo with the college orchestra. This was not a requirement for graduation, but it was an honor, and her father and grandparents were flying in early to attend. Isabel had chosen to play Mozart's Piano Concerto Number 21, which would be the main work in the second half of the program. She had taken a course on the history of film and admired the movie *Elvira Madigan* that told the story of two doomed lovers. The soundtrack for the film was this particular Mozart concerto. Isabel decided not to share that information with her music professors, believing they would be unimpressed by the reason for her choice.

Alice had called George to plead with him to take some vacation days, so that he could go to the concert and then stay through graduation the following week. His flight was due to arrive the morning of the day of Isabel's afternoon concert. Alice planned that they would meet briefly beforehand, that she and her parents and George

WHILE THE MUSIC LASTS

would attend the performance and that, afterward, they and Isabel's relatives would all go out to dinner in Philadelphia.

Three hours before the concert, George called Alice.

"I'm still in New York. There have been bad thunderstorms delaying everything. The weather's improving but my flight also has a maintenance problem. That's all they'll tell us, and they won't even estimate our departure time."

Alice tried to keep her deep disappointment out of her voice, but this was not easy since she wanted so much for George to hear Isabel play. She paused.

George said, "Sis, are you still there?"

Alice replied, "Yes. Look, whatever happens, you will have to come directly to the Lang Music Building on campus. I'll wait for you at the entrance. Do you have a pen? I'll give you directions so you can tell the taxi driver where to take you when you get to the college."

The first half of the concert was just ending when George arrived. Alice and he waited at the door to the hall until they heard applause, then they slipped in quietly and sat high in the back.

George found himself looking down on a stage where the orchestra was rising and leaving for intermission. A grand piano was being rolled into place. In the background there were very tall floor-to-ceiling windows that overlooked trees and the dense foliage next to Crum Creek.

Alice heard her brother catch his breath at his first sight of Isabel. Tall, pale and slender, her abundant red hair swept up into a French knot, she was wearing an elegantly simple, long black dress. As she began to play, Alice relaxed back in her seat, throwing sideways glances at George who remained leaning forward. She took it to be

WHILE THE MUSIC LASTS

a good sign that George never did sit back throughout the rest of the concert. He watched as if transfixed.

For his part, George could hardly believe what he was seeing and hearing. Here was this lovely creature his sister had told him about, but nothing in her description had prepared him for the presence of Isabel. She moved with infinite grace and seemed to play almost effortlessly what he knew, in reality, to be a difficult piece.

Alice had told George that Isabel was delightful, and he had sensed that his sister's matchmaking mode was running at full tilt. But now he was incredibly grateful and wanted nothing less than a full introduction to this beautiful woman who had such a delicacy about her that he instinctively began to feel protective toward her.

Alice had not told George about Isabel's breakdown. There were confidences she felt she could not share even with George. It was up to Isabel to reveal these as she alone saw fit. But, in some way, George did not need to be told. He knew that he very much wanted to meet Isabel and, at the same time, he felt uncharacteristically shy about the impending introduction.

The concert was a great success and, when it was over, Isabel was surrounded by friends waiting to congratulate her. Finally she caught the eye of her father and grandparents who were standing a little to the side. She beamed at them and began to inch toward them. She had very nearly reached them before she was aware of Alice and of a man who had to be Alice's brother standing off to her right. She recognized him at once, as he was, in all respects, a male version of Alice. He was tall, well over six feet, and had his sister's coloring: white blonde hair and pale blue eyes. He reminded Isabel of a character in an Ingmar Bergman film.

WHILE THE MUSIC LASTS

Introductions were made all around, and the assembled relatives gathered in two cars to drive to a restaurant in Philadelphia.

Alice was determined to have Isabel sit next to her brother at dinner, and the seating arrangements fell into place naturally. Isabel and George were beside each other and Alice, though she was fully prepared to do so, had not been obliged to make an issue of it.

Isabel tried to put George at ease. She was aware that, although he did his best to conceal it, he was shy with her.

"Alice told me that you are serving your first church. Are you enjoying the work – is it everything that you expected?"

"Yes, and then some," George replied. "I'm camping out in what will be the associate minister's parsonage. The church bought the place a few months ago, and it needs a lot of work. Eventually there will be a committee to do renovation and redecorating. But there are more important matters on the church's calendar right now, so it may be awhile."

"It's amazing what can be done sometimes with just fresh paint and relatively inexpensive fabrics. I enjoy some of those makeover features they have in design magazines," Isabel said.

"I'm hopeless at that sort of thing," George answered, "but I'll bet some of the parish women will have good ideas. Anyway, you were asking if the work is all I'd hoped."

Isabel nodded.

"There is a nice family living two doors down from me. They're in our church and the wife was expecting her second child. One day in February we had a heavy snowstorm, almost a blizzard. That night I heard a loud banging on my front door at two a.m. It was the husband. His wife was in labor, and he couldn't get his car started. He knew I had a station wagon. So I drove them as fast as I dared on the snow and ice, and we got to the hospital just in time. I guess you could say that was my first 'good deed' as a minister."

"Wow!" Isabel exclaimed. "I'd call that 'baptism by fire' or 'by snowstorm'!"

They laughed and George slowly began to unbend. The more they spoke, the more comfortable he became.

"Did Alice tell you that I just made it to your concert in time to hear you play? My plane was delayed, and I didn't get there until intermission. You were marvelous. I'm so happy I didn't miss hearing you."

"Thank you. I'm glad you enjoyed it," Isabel smiled.

"Where will you spend your summer?" George asked.

"My grandparents live in upstate New York, and I have always spent my summers with them." Isabel smiled at her father and grandparents who were busily conversing at the opposite side of the table. "They want me back again this year. In fact, they have told me I can make my home with them for as long as I like. They know how much I enjoy being with them; I've spent some of my happiest days there." Isabel hesitated. She looked into George's eyes that were gentle as they watched her intently. She had a sudden impulse to tell him about her worst days there, about Jean-Marc, about her mother's death, about how being there would always be bittersweet from now on. But she barely knew him, and she believed he would think her quite mad if she began telling him all of this. She wondered how much Alice had told him about her, and she was suddenly and inexplicably certain that Alice had divulged very little. Alice, she thought, simply would not give away her secrets – even to her own brother. She cleared her throat and continued.

"Of course, if I do decide to live there, I would want to work at something. My grandmother has a baby grand piano. She's suggested that I could use it and give piano lessons. My grandparents live in a small town with a weekly newspaper. If I advertise in it, grandmother thinks I might find enough pupils to keep me busy."

George started to say something more but everyone had finished dessert, and there was a general pushing back of chairs while napkins were deposited on the table.

As they were walking toward their cars, George asked, "Does your father live in New York state too?" He was watching Isabel's father who was walking half a block in front of them.

"My dad lives in New York City… in the same apartment where I grew up. There was some talk of having him move to a smaller place after my mother died and I went off to college. But we soon sensed that he wasn't that keen to leave. The apartment holds a lot of happy memories for him. A cleaning lady comes in once a week, but he enjoys puttering about the place and keeping everything neat. He's a mechanical engineer, and he's always been interested in details – in having everything just right."

"Do you inherit your musical talent from him?"

"Both of my parents loved music, and they often took me to concerts when they thought I was old enough. My mother played a little but, no, my dad doesn't."

"Well," George smiled, "you've inherited some very talented genes from someone!"

Isabel and Alice both received high honors. During senior week, George invited Isabel to spend the day with

WHILE THE MUSIC LASTS

him at Longwood Gardens. The weather was beautiful as they strolled around the grounds full of magnificent flower beds and neatly manicured lawns, pausing occasionally to sit on shaded benches. They talked easily and found that they shared many things in common. George could see that Isabel was serious but in no way self-important. She had a streak of charming, self-deprecating humor that he found delightful.

Isabel thoroughly enjoyed the day with George. She could not help liking him. He had all of Alice's enthusiasm for life, and Isabel sensed he was confident in his chosen calling. He appeared to enjoy counseling people and guiding them as best he could in what he considered the right direction. Isabel appreciated the fact that there seemed to be nothing remotely judgmental in his manner. Alice had told Isabel that George was very forthright, and she observed this to be true. More and more, she thought he resembled the Swedish actor, Max von Sydow. Without mentioning this to him, she nevertheless brought up the subject of film and of Ingmar Bergman. She told George that she had taken a course on the history of film and had written a paper on the Swedish director. She was pleasantly surprised when George said that Bergman's films had long intrigued him, especially *Winter Light* about a clergyman and the silence of God. He and Isabel discussed the imagery and the bleakness of Bergman's philosophy.

Isabel remarked that she thought *Winter Light* was one of Bergman's starkest works and that, perhaps, the most haunting line in the film is when the clergyman says, "It was my parents who wanted me to go into the church."

"He admits that he became a minister without the vocation," Isabel said. She paused and smiled at George saying, "I'm certain you feel no similar compunction?"

George laughed, "No, not at all." Then, more seriously, "What did you make of the film's ending?"

"I remember a book I read about that by John Simon. He said, if I recall the quote correctly, Bergman is saying that it's not 'a question of God being love and vice versa… only of aloneness being shareable and so making life endurable,' that 'hell together is better than hell alone.'"

"Do you believe that?" George asked.

Isabel thought a moment. "Yes, although I think I'm a bit more optimistic than Bergman in that I hope God's love fits into the equation somehow."

They walked on for a while without speaking. Isabel felt George looking at her and, when she glanced at him, he smiled. In the bright sunlight, she was struck once again by his resemblance to Alice. They shared the same finely chiseled features, fair skin and piercing blue eyes, and both had the tow-colored hair often associated with children but rarely seen in adults. Isabel thought George was almost too handsome, but the wariness she usually experienced with very good-looking men – a hesitancy occasioned by the fear that they would be thoroughly egotistical – was lacking with George. She felt drawn to him, and she liked the fact that they could walk together, quietly and comfortably, as if they had known each other far longer, as if they were old friends.

Isabel finally broke the silence by mentioning Bergman's occasional use of color. She asked George if he knew the film *Cries and Whispers*. She said Bergman's first hint of that story came to him when he imagined a red room inhabited by women in white dresses.

George said, "It's a magnificent film but I found some of the last scenes – where the woman is dying – really hard to watch. What is the character's name – the one who dies?"

"Agnes… the character's name is Agnes. Harriet Andersson is the actress who plays her."

"Well, she certainly portrays suffering realistically… a little too realistically for me."

"Yes, she's very believable, and I see what you're saying, but I think the film has some religious overtones. Bergman said that, for him, the color red represents 'the interior of the soul.' And the viewer can take Agnes' suffering to be almost Christ-like."

"Ahh… yes, I hadn't thought of it in that way," George replied.

Toward the end of the afternoon, as they were walking out of the gardens, George took Isabel's hand and said, "I'd like to write to you this summer. If I write, will you answer me?"

Isabel was flattered, "Yes, it would be nice to hear from you."

As they were saying goodbye, George leaned down and kissed her on the cheek.

When Alice learned that Isabel and her brother would be corresponding, she smiled to herself; inside, she was elated. Isabel, sensing this, decided not to mention the kiss.

Thinking about Isabel during his trip back to Connecticut, George believed, at least he fervently hoped, that he had met his future wife. In addition to letters, he began sending cards to her at her grandparents. Because she had once mentioned that she loved animals, he sent cards with photographs of cute puppies or kittens. Sometimes, he sent cards that made her laugh. Their sense of humor seemed to be much the same. He chose nothing ribald or even vaguely obscene. He also never found funny any sarcastic, disparaging jokes at the expense of other people. Isabel liked that about him. If she were asked to describe his personality, she would have said he was not only nice, but thoroughly decent.

Near the end of June, Isabel was just finishing breakfast when the telephone rang. Her grandmother answered it in the kitchen and called out, "Isabel, it's for you. It's Alice Larsson."

Isabel quickly deposited her dishes in the sink. The phone was on the desk where cookbooks were lined against the wall, held in place by bookends in the form of lions. These splendid, reclining creatures had always fascinated Isabel as a child, and her grandmother had told her that they were small replicas of stone lions at Chatsworth, a stately home in England.

Isabel eagerly picked up the receiver and, hearing her friend's familiar voice, she realized how much she had missed her. "It's so good to hear from you," she said, absent-mindedly rubbing her finger over the mane of one of the lions.

After an exchange of pleasantries, Alice said, "I'm calling because, in a couple of weeks, George and I are going to spend a long weekend at our uncle's cottage in the foothills of the Poconos. It's on Lake Windsor, which is about forty minutes south of Binghamton. I know that's close to your neck of the woods, and we're hoping you might be free to join us."

"That would be lovely!" Isabel exclaimed, looking at the desk calendar. "Do you mean the weekend of the fourteenth?"

"Yes, we could come and pick you up."

"If you're going south of Binghamton, it would be nearly an hour out of your way to come here. My grandmother

WHILE THE MUSIC LASTS

goes to Binghamton about every week to do some shopping. It might be that she could drop me off there. Just a minute; let me check with her."

After a brief conversation with her grandmother, Isabel was back on the line. "Nana says that will be fine. Thanks so much, Alice!"

"Where shall we meet in Binghamton?"

"Hmm, let's see... I probably should stand in front of the Press Building. I'll send you a map and a description. Don't worry; anyone in Binghamton will know where the Press Building is if you should get lost."

"Okay, and we'll bring you home. Shall we meet around ten the morning of the fourteenth?"

"Yes, fine."

"Oh, be sure to pack a sweater. It can be chilly even in July."

"I will – and thanks again."

The night of the thirteenth there was wind, lightning and torrential rain. Isabel half woke several times to the sound of thunder. But the next morning dawned clear with brilliant sunshine and the air had the unique freshness that frequently follows a severe storm. A few small branches had blown down, and her grandfather was busy collecting these into a pile as Isabel and her grandmother emerged from the house and walked down the driveway toward the car. Isabel ran to him, giving him a hug and kiss as she said, "Goodbye, Grandpa. We're off to Binghamton."

"The forecast is for sunny skies the next three days," he replied. "Have a great weekend!"

As they left the driveway, Nana indicated a plastic sack she had put on the seat next to Isabel. "That's for you to take," she said, "to give to your hostess."

Isabel looked inside. "A loaf of your zucchini bread! Oh, Nana, you think of everything."

Isabel planned to arrive in Binghamton with considerable time to spare, but she had been waiting in front of the Press Building for only about ten minutes when Alice and George pulled up in George's station wagon. Mindful of the traffic, Isabel quickly opened the back door, threw her small suitcase on the seat and got in. George took the time to reach around to shake her hand as Alice leaned over the back of the passenger seat to embrace her.

"This is so nice!" Isabel said. "And my grandfather said the forecast is for three beautiful days, so we're lucky. We had a hard rain last night."

"I'm glad to hear the weather is supposed to cooperate," George answered. "It can be very dreary at the lake cottage when it rains."

"You said this is your uncle's cottage?" Isabel inquired.

"It belongs to our father's older brother, John, and his wife Moira," Alice explained. "He's retired. He was a chemist and his wife is an artist. She does book illustrations, that sort of thing."

"They spend their summers at the lake and their winters on the west coast of Florida. The two places couldn't be more different," George said. "I'd say the Florida condo is sophisticated, wouldn't you, Alice, and the cottage is…?"

"Homey," Alice replied. "Comfortable and homey."

"Right," George agreed.

The three of them chatted and laughed and caught up on each other's news as they gradually left the city behind them and crossed the border into Pennsylvania. Before long they started up a steep hill, and Alice said, "This is the road that leads to the lake. When George and I were kids, it was just a dirt road that they oiled to keep the dust down. I remember, when it was sunny, being fascinated by the different colors in the tiny pools of oil. They don't use oil anymore, of course, but people didn't seem to care that much about the environment then."

They reached the crest of the hill, and Isabel had her first view of the dark blue, spring-fed lake surrounded by a forest of evergreens with cottages nestled among the pines. The properties each seemed to have at least an acre of land.

George pulled up in front of a white-shingled house with a gabled second floor. There was a columned front porch that stretched the width of the house. A row of white rocking chairs with dark green seat cushions beckoned. But the feature that distinguished this cottage from all of the others was the small clearing in front. There the owners had planted a garden of riotous blooms: dahlias, hollyhocks, impatiens and other lush flowers, some of which were unfamiliar to Isabel. There were two birdhouses, one painted white with a red roof and the other red with a white roof. A birdbath was in the middle of the garden and a birdfeeder hung nearby.

"Oh, how absolutely charming!" Isabel exclaimed.

"Our aunt and uncle like to garden," Alice said modestly as she was getting out of the station wagon.

"And bird watch," George added, unlatching the back.

The door of the cottage opened and a petite, dark-haired woman and a tall, lanky man with thinning sandy hair and a full mustache came down the path to greet them.

Alice and George hugged their aunt and uncle and introduced Isabel.

"Welcome!" the man said, shaking Isabel's hand warmly. Observing him as he took her suitcase from her, Isabel could see that he shared the Larsson family's blue eyes and that his had a decided twinkle. Isabel liked him at once.

Aunt Moira's dark hair complimented her very fair skin and green eyes. Isabel guessed that her ancestry was Celtic, a guess strengthened later when she saw a small landscape in the bedroom signed "Moira Ryan Larsson."

Isabel walked across a slab at the bottom of the porch steps with the words "Pax Vobiscum" etched into it.

"Peace be with you," she murmured. "That's nice."

"My uncle has a good story about it. Ask him at lunch," George replied.

"Please come in," Moira said, stepping aside to allow Isabel to enter the living room.

"We've put you and Alice in the room at the back with the twin beds. If you'll just follow me…"

But Isabel seemed rooted to the spot. She was staring at a large reproduction of a watercolor above the fireplace. The painting was of a little girl watering several plants on a sill underneath a long window. The child's blonde hair was fashioned in a single braid down her back, and she was wearing a blue dress. In the foreground was a white table where knitting, needles and a ball of yarn had been left. Along with a white chest of drawers, a white Swedish-style chair with a blue and white striped seat was to the right. The pale walls were covered with plain panels edged in green.

"Oh," Moira said, hesitating. "I see you like our Carl Larsson."

"Carl Larsson?"

"The watercolor over the mantel is a reproduction of

WHILE THE MUSIC LASTS

a Carl Larsson. It's called *The Flower Window*." When Isabel failed to respond, Moira went on, "He was a Swedish artist who lived from 1853 until 1919."

Isabel said, "Larsson? Was he an ancestor?"

Moira smiled. "John likes to think we might be distantly related, although there's absolutely no proof."

"But you've copied the room!" Isabel said, looking around her at the white furniture and the chairs and sofa upholstered in blue and white stripes. The walls echoed the panels edged in green and just to Isabel's right was a sun porch with a long window with numerous plants on the sill beneath. "It's even the same window!" Isabel exclaimed. "It's exactly the same!"

Moira said, " When we bought this place there was a rather ugly jalousie window out there so we had it replaced. Not many people notice that, but yes, you're right. I asked the contractor to copy the one in the painting."

"I told you Isabel was clever, didn't I?" Alice asked, smiling.

"Come and see where we eat, then," George urged.

The dining room had another large reproduction of a Carl Larsson on the most prominent wall. The picture was of a nineteenth-century woman and two children in a dining room with high, green wainscoting and an oak trestle table. The children were beside a cupboard with glass panes, and the woman was standing in front of a sideboard. Both of these pieces were painted reddish orange. Moira had duplicated the color on two very similar pieces of furniture.

"It took us a while to find these," Moira explained, indicating the cupboard and the sideboard. "We went to a lot of flea markets."

"And you found the oak table and used the same

wainscoting too."

"Yes, exactly."

"I've never seen anything remotely like this," Isabel said. "It's absolutely lovely!"

During a pause in the conversation at lunch, Isabel remembered to ask her host about the story concerning the "Pax Vobiscum" inscription at the entrance.

"I found that quite by chance," John said. "I was driving by a site where an old mansion was being demolished. Off to one side, the contractors were selling bits and pieces of the architecture. I saw the slab and thought it would be nice to use as the last stone of the path leading to the cottage. It hadn't been installed very long when a traveling salesman came to the door and inquired if he might speak to 'Mr. or Mrs. Vobiscum.' I had all I could do to keep from saying, 'Oh, please, just call me 'Pax.'"

Isabel burst into laughter. "You're not serious?" she asked finally.

"Yes, totally serious," John said, smiling.

"John was having such a hard time keeping a straight face that I had to shove him out of the way. And I actually bought some of the man's brushes or whatever it was he was selling because I felt guilty at being amused at his expense," Moira explained.

After lunch Alice and Isabel helped Moira clear the table and then joined George who was standing on their dock. Below them, a rowboat was anchored among some lily pads.

"Anyone for an excursion?" George asked. "I'll row."

When they had nearly reached the center of the lake, George rested and they floated for a while. Alice pointed out three white buildings on the opposite shore. "Those are for the church camp. The children come for two weeks each summer. The girls' dorm is on the right; the boys' dorm is on the left, and the dining hall is in the middle. George and I and our cousins went there as kids. It's where the Larssons first became aware of this lake and decided to summer here."

"You didn't like camp as much as I did," George said to Alice. "You used to complain about having to get up so early."

"Yes, I was always fast asleep when the bugle sounded at six thirty in the morning. The counselors immediately made us go out to get our bathing suits off the line and the suits were cold and damp with dew. To add insult to injury, they then made us swim laps in the lake before breakfast. All of that was definitely not my cup of tea."

"Oh, my poor, delicate little sister…" George teased.

"Delicate, nothing!" Alice retorted. "We really got you boys that one time…"

"I'll say!" George responded with mock indignation. "Do you know what the girls did when they knew we boys were out of our dorm? They went in and tied our sheets into knots – including the counselor's!"

"Well," Alice said, looking down, "you got your revenge."

"Of course we did!" George replied.

"What happened? What did you do?" Isabel asked.

"There used to be a bait and tackle shop just before you turned on to the lake road," George said. " We went there and bought some rubber worms, some rubber nightcrawlers. At breakfast we fixed it with the counselor that he would say an extra long grace, and, during that, we put the worms in the girls' glasses of tomato juice. One girl actually got a worm in her mouth, and all of them screamed!'

"So," Alice said, "just in case you think George was a

goody two shoes, the angelic little cherub who would grow up to become a saintly minister…"

"I've outgrown such pranks," George remarked.

"Oh, really," Alice said archly looking at George. "Do tell!"

George frowned at Alice and started to reply, but evidently thought better of it.

That evening before dinner, as they were enjoying drinks on the porch, Isabel heard music coming from the lake:

"Way down upon the Swanee River, far, far away…"

As she looked, she saw a replica of a Mississippi River paddleboat rounding the bend. The boat was rimmed with lights and patriotic red, white and blue bunting.

"Oh!" Isabel exclaimed with delight.

"That's the Dixie," Alice said. "She goes around the lake each evening, giving rides and playing Stephen Foster songs. When it gets dark, if you flash your exterior lights, the captain will blow her horn in response."

"What fun!" Isabel said, watching intensely as the boat neared.

"Aunt Moira," Alice remarked, "George was telling us earlier today that he has outgrown his love of childish pranks, but, as I recall, on the fourth of July last year…"

Moira took the bait and, to Alice's great satisfaction, said, "Outgrown! George how can you say that?" Turning to Isabel, she continued, "Don't let anyone tell you that Larsson men ever outgrow pranks! Last year John and George got a toy cannon, and John used his knowledge of chemistry to cook up some concoction. When the Dixie was directly opposite our house, he and George lit it and there was a huge boom followed by a large cloud of

WHILE THE MUSIC LASTS

billowing black smoke. The poor Dixie actually veered off course, going farther out into the lake. She never came close to shore here for the rest of the evening!"

John gave a small smile of satisfaction at the memory while George simply looked chagrined.

George was quiet at dinner. As they were finishing dessert, they heard the Dixie approaching again. Alice, fearing she might have gone too far in teasing George, suggested that he show Isabel how to flash the light.

"Would you like to see?" he asked Isabel.

"I'd love to!" she replied.

They rose and went into the living room.

"Go out on the porch," George said. As Isabel closed the door behind her, he flashed the light at the end of the path several times, and the Dixie tooted twice in response. George joined her on the porch, and together they watched the boat recede into the distance.

"Would you like to take a ride on her tomorrow, after dinner?" George asked.

"Oh, yes, definitely!" Isabel replied. "And, by the way, I think pranks can be fun. Growing up completely is just plain boring." She smiled at him as he put his arm around her waist.

The next morning after breakfast, Alice suggested that they pack a picnic lunch and go for a bicycle ride around the lake. Alice and Isabel went scrounging in the refrigerator and found some cold cuts, hard-boiled eggs, bread, fruit and soft drinks. Freshly baked brownies and oatmeal cookies were on the counter.

"Take whatever you like," Moira said. "Two of the bikes have baskets. Let me put some ice into a plastic bag for the things that should be kept cold, and I think we have…" She stood on tiptoe, peering into a cupboard. "Yes, here they are," she murmured as she brought out plastic plates and paper napkins. Turning to George, she said, "If you look on the top shelf in the pantry, you'll find an old picnic blanket."

Alice, Isabel and George started off shortly before eleven. The day was warm and clear with a soft, cool breeze rippling across the lake. Alice and George waved at neighbors as they passed the various cottages. None was quite as lovely as the Larssons', Isabel thought.

When they reached the halfway point, George, who was leading, pulled over and stopped. "Down there is a good place," he said. "Do you see that flat spot on the grass next to the water?" They left their bikes propped against some trees and carried their provisions down to the lake. They spread out the blanket and sat under the pines looking across the water. At the far end of the lake was a large house painted a dark green, and they could see the Dixie moored at a landing in front of it.

"That green house is the clubhouse now. It was the home of the original owner," Alice said. "All of this land once belonged to him. After he died, his family sold it, and it was divided up to become this summer colony."

"It's certainly an idyllic place," Isabel said, "with the lake surrounded by these beautiful pines."

"There's a story about the trees," George said. "Back in the thirties when the first cottages were being built, the government was doing a reforestation project. The new owners decided to order some trees and were slated to receive a large number – some hundreds of evergreens. They enlisted the help of a lot of farmers in the area. Anyone who had a truck and was willing to haul trees up to the lake was welcome. They waited at the station; the train pulled in; the freight door opened… and boxes of three or four inch seedlings were handed out… not exactly the 'trees' they had in mind."

Isabel smiled. George stretched and stood up. He went to the water's edge, picked up a flat stone and expertly skipped it across the water.

"How do you do that?" Isabel asked. "I can never get a stone to skip."

"Come here and I'll show you." George stood behind her and demonstrated how she should hold her wrist. After a few failures, Isabel managed a couple of skips. "Yes!" she exclaimed happily.

John grilled fish he had caught early that morning for dinner, and Moira made corn muffins, a green bean casserole and a custard cream pie. They ate leisurely, watching the sunset over the lake. The sky was a brilliant orange and pink.

"Isabel," George said, "I think we should drive down to the landing and get on the Dixie for her next run around the lake. Will you excuse us, everyone?" George took pains to make it clear that he wanted to be alone with Isabel. The others accepted this gracefully and, though George could not know it, with pleasure.

As they stepped on board the Dixie, George said, "Let's go up. It's fun to be on top where it's open and we can see the stars." They sat on a seat near the front as the boat cast off her ropes and the music began.

"My Old Kentucky Home…"

"This has been a marvelous weekend, George," Isabel said. "I'll never forget it."

"I won't either," he said as he put his arm around her. She rested her head on his shoulder as they looked up at

WHILE THE MUSIC LASTS

the moon and the constellations. George kissed her on the forehead, and Isabel thought how very comfortable she felt with him, how very safe.

When Isabel returned to her grandparents, George began calling her several times a week and they had long, involved conversations. After they had not seen each other for six weeks, George hesitantly asked a question. Isabel could tell that he was trying to keep his tone casual, but she sensed her answer would be important to him.

"I was wondering," he said, "if it might be possible for me to come and see you? I have a few days off next week."

Isabel was surprised but quickly said yes.

"Is there a decent motel in the vicinity?"

"Oh, no," Isabel replied. "I mean you mustn't stay in a motel. My grandparents will want you to stay here."

"I'd be imposing – "

"No, you wouldn't. You saw how big this house is when you brought me home from the lake. It was built in the nineteenth century when people had large families and servants. We have tons of room."

"If you're sure." George sounded relieved.

"Absolutely!" Isabel replied.

She wondered if he intended to propose to her, and she began to think of what she would say if he did. She knew that she would have to be completely honest with him about her feelings. She was exceedingly fond of him. She believed she could even say she loved him although she felt no overwhelming passion for him. She would explain, without going into details, about Jean-Marc, and she would tell him that she thought she was incapable of ever loving so heedlessly again. She would let him know how much her mother's sudden death had affected her, and she would tell him about the mental hospital, and about the insomnia that still plagued her occasionally.

Isabel's grandparents were pleased that George was coming. They liked him at once when they first met at graduation. He arrived shortly after dinner and, once the greetings and initial pleasantries were over, he and Isabel withdrew to the screened porch. They sat side by side on the wicker loveseat. In the twilight, they remained silent for a few minutes. Isabel watched as the cheerful floral chintz cushions faded into the encroaching darkness. She leaned over to turn on a lamp and smiled at George. He reached over and took her hand.

"I think you may know why I'm here," he said.

Isabel nodded and answered softly, "Yes."

"I've fallen very much in love with you and I... I've come to ask you to be my wife."

Isabel took both of George's hands in hers and began to speak quietly and very earnestly. It took her some time to express all of her thoughts, and he listened to her without interrupting. After she finished telling him about her stay in the mental hospital, she paused.

George squeezed her hands gently and said "Oh, Isabel, I'm so sorry you had to go through all of that."

"Does it matter?" she whispered. "I mean, can you still care for me knowing I've been in a psychiatric hospital? There is still a stigma attached..."

"Of course, I still care about you! Nothing you have told me has changed my feelings for you, except perhaps to strengthen them."

Isabel sat back; she sighed and was quiet for a few moments. Realizing that her silence must be weighing on George, she finally asked, "Would you mind terribly if

I give you my answer tomorrow? The delay has nothing to do with you. It's all to do with me. I think I can be a good minister's wife, but I need to examine my religious convictions very carefully. Church has always been a part of my life, but if I marry you, it will become a central part. I think we need to talk further... I think you should hear my views about religion. And I need to have tonight to organize my thoughts, so they don't come out in a hopeless muddle."

George leaned forward and gave her a hug. "Yes, of course," he said. "We'll talk in the morning."

The next day dawned perfectly clear with a cloudless blue sky and temperatures that were to reach into the high seventies. Isabel came down carrying a book and found George and her grandparents just sitting down to breakfast. Her grandmother had outdone herself with poached eggs and a homemade cinnamon pecan coffee cake. When George and Isabel commented on how delicious everything was, Nana said, "In my experience, bachelors always enjoy a good home-cooked breakfast."

Isabel glanced at George then looked down and blushed.

George smiled and said, "And you're absolutely right about that, too."

After breakfast, Isabel asked George if he would like to walk down and see the river. As they stood on the bank she said, "I used to be terrified of this river because I dropped a ball into it when I was small, and my mother was afraid I was going in after it. She shrieked and grabbed me, and I associated her fear with the water."

George put an arm around Isabel's shoulder, and they sat on the cool grass under the shade of a large oak. Isabel said, "I thought a lot about my beliefs last night, and how

WHILE THE MUSIC LASTS

I could express them. First off, I do, of course, believe in God – in a Creator. I can't think that all we know of music, literature, art and science happened simply by chance. There's so much richness and beauty and complexity that I believe creation was more than some haphazard event. The fact that life exists at all seems to be very finely calibrated. I knew there was a quote that summarizes a lot of what I think and, last night, in the middle of the night I went down to the library to search for it. It's by a scientist, Stephen Jay Gould, who certainly isn't a Christian apologist or even a theist…" Isabel handed George the book she had brought down to breakfast. "Here, I've marked the page."

George took the book and began to read.

"Something almost unspeakably holy - I don't know how else to say this - underlies our discovery and confirmation of the actual details that made our world and also, in realms of contingency, assured the minutiae of its construction in the manner we know, and not in any one of a trillion other ways, nearly all of which would not have included the evolution of a scribe to record the beauty, the cruelty, the fascination and the mystery."

"That's well stated," George said.

"It is, isn't it?" Isabel answered.

"The only change I would make would be to leave out the word 'almost' before 'unspeakably holy'."

Isabel thought for a moment then nodded her head saying, "Yes, I agree."

They were silent for a while, listening to the birds' constant twittering and watching the great river as it moved swiftly past them.

"This certainly is a beautiful spot," George said.

"Yes," Isabel agreed. "Now you can understand why I love it here so much. Sitting here you can almost forget your own and the world's problems. Only, it's not possible ever to ignore them completely." Isabel lay back on her elbows and stretched out her legs. "Theology is concerned with the problem of evil, isn't it?"

"Absolutely, it's a very basic problem."

"I have some further thoughts," Isabel went on, "but I'm almost ashamed to voice them because you know so much more about all of this than I do."

"Please go on; tell me what you think," George encouraged her.

"Well, I see the world as a school, and I think humanity can only appreciate true goodness if it experiences its opposite. I don't have a problem with the concept of free will but where the Christian idea of Jesus is concerned, I think I don't exactly follow doctrine."

"How do you mean?" George asked.

"I can believe that Jesus was a Son of God, but I'm not persuaded He was the only Son of God. I think most religions are attempts to reach the Almighty and that each has its own validity. I even question religion altogether when it becomes an excuse for divisiveness and cruelty."

"That's perfectly understandable."

"Really?"

"Yes," George smiled and gave a slight chuckle. Seeing Isabel frown, he hastened to explain that he was not laughing at her. "I was remembering my own problems with doctrine when I was at Oxford. The rector there helped me a lot. If you'd like, I can tell you what he said." He paused while Isabel nodded her head. " I mean, the fact is that I can debate doctrine with you until the cows come home. But nothing you've said so far shocks me. Is there more?"

Isabel looked down and then said almost shyly, "I've

always hoped to be married one day and have a family of my own. I guess I've laid everything about myself out for you to see. If you still want to marry me, warts and all, then my answer is yes."

George's face flushed with joy and, when Isabel looked at him, his eyes were dancing. He started to speak but could only manage "I... I..."

Isabel smiled at him and said, "I did say yes."

"I know. You've made me so happy!" He stood up and pulled her up beside him before drawing her to him and kissing her. He hugged her and whispered, "I love you." Holding her at arms length to look at her, he could scarcely believe she would be his wife. Isabel appeared serious. To reassure her he smiled and said, "We'll make a great team."

Isabel laughed. "Yes, I think we very well might."

They were somewhat breathless and obviously happy when they rejoined Isabel's grandparents and told them the news. Isabel immediately called her father in New York, and George phoned his parents and Alice. All were overjoyed, and none more so than Andrew who learned the news the next day. Rising early, Isabel saw him in his garden potting some flowers. She put on her robe as she dashed down the stairs barefoot and ran out the back door.

"Andy!" she called. "Andy, I have something important to tell you!"

Andrew stood up, left what he was doing and walked toward her.

"I'm getting married!" she called out.

"What?"

"I'm getting married – to George Larsson – my college roommate's brother," she repeated and watched as he smiled broadly.

"Great!" he exclaimed. "Congratulations!" He swept her off her feet as he gave her a hug and twirled her around. "You deserve every happiness, Isabel," he said, putting her down. "After all you've been through, this was worth waiting for, wasn't it? Whoever George is, he's a very lucky man! When do I get to meet him?"

"He's here. He's still asleep. Come to lunch and I'll introduce you." Looking down, she continued, "I'm lucky too, Andy. He's awfully nice. You'll see."

―――

Isabel's grandmother began discussing wedding plans immediately. "You always said you would like to be married here someday. We could have the ceremony in the garden or in front of the fireplace in the living room if the weather fails to cooperate…" Seeing Isabel's face, she stopped.

Isabel spoke hesitantly. "Nana, would you mind terribly if we didn't get married here? I think George would like to have a church wedding, but there's more to it than that. I know you and Mother and I always used to talk about my being married here one day… but that's just it, you see. I really don't want to use this house or garden since Mother can't be here. It's probably foolish of me, but this occasion was supposed to be her big day too. She would have loved so much planning a large wedding down to the last detail, and, well, I just don't want an elaborate wedding without her."

Nana motioned Isabel to come and sit beside her. "Of course, I understand what you're feeling, darling. And I think you're absolutely right."

"Truly? I don't want to disappoint you."

"Don't you worry about that," Nana said, patting her hand.

George and Isabel decided on a small wedding in George's church with the senior minister officiating. Only their closest relatives and friends were invited.

Alice went with Isabel to help her choose a wedding dress and find her own maid of honor's outfit. They giggled like two children at the absurdity of some of the dresses and veils. Isabel decided on a long, elegantly tailored white dress with three-quarter length sleeves and a rounded neck. It was free of adornment and she planned to wear her mother's single strand of pearls with matching pearl button earrings. They agreed that a veil would be too formal and eventually chose a white picture hat trimmed with ivory silk roses.

Isabel helped Alice decide on her dress as well. They liked both a pale pink lace and an ice blue chiffon. After some discussion, they took the blue. The fact that the color matched Alice's eyes helped settle the matter.

The wedding day dawned bright and clear with only a slightly chilly breeze from the north. Everything went as planned. Isabel and the church organist, a Mrs. Wilde, had chosen the music together. George had, as he called it, a "tin ear" and usually mouthed the words of hymns or sang very softly for fear of being off key.

Mrs. Wilde asked if Isabel would like the traditional Mendelssohn wedding march, and Isabel decided that would be best. They chose some works of Shubert and Bach, including the *Air for the G String.* The only break with custom was the hymn, "Providence," which was to the melody of Jean Sibelius' *Finlandia.* Isabel included it because it had been her mother's favorite hymn. Since

it was played before Isabel came down the aisle on her father's arm, no one was expected to sing it, and Isabel doubted that many would know the words that she knew were inappropriate for a wedding:
>Be still, my soul: the Lord is on thy side;
>Bear patiently the cross of grief or pain;
>Leave to thy God to order and provide;
>In every change He faithful will remain.
>Be still, my soul: thy best thy heavenly Friend
>Thro' thorny ways leads to a joyful end.

Aunt Moira and Uncle John made the penthouse condominium they owned in Florida on Longboat Key, available to the newlyweds for their honeymoon. After the wedding, at the reception, which was held at the town's only hotel, Andrew heartily shook George's hand and told him how fortunate he was. There were many hugs and farewells before Isabel's father drove her and George to Hartford to catch a plane for Tampa. They landed at three thirty in the afternoon after an uneventful flight. George left Isabel with the luggage and went to pick up the rental car they had reserved in advance, and they then began the hour's drive to the island.

Isabel had never been to Florida before, and, that day, it deserved its name as the "Sunshine State." The sky was blue and cloudless and palm fronds waved in a gentle breeze. After forty-five minutes, they left route 41 and drove west toward the city of Bradenton. Isabel said, "Look at that Episcopal church – and did you notice the bank in the previous block? I love the Spanish style architecture… the bright colors and those orange tile roofs are wonderful!"

As they started across the causeway leading to Longboat Key, Isabel exclaimed, "Look! Look!" A pelican and several seagulls were flying nearby. George smiled at her enthusiasm.

They drove on the island's large, central boulevard, passing several high-rise condominiums until George signaled a right turn into a parking lot. "This is the one," he said. "We have to go up to the twelfth floor."

Isabel gasped as George unlocked the condominium's double doors then picked her up to carry her across the threshold. Moira had seen to it that the cleaning lady opened the apartment, making everything perfect for them. A fresh bouquet of pink roses was on the coffee table. The condominium's living room, dining room and master bedroom all had floor-to-ceiling windows fronting directly on the Gulf. The floor-length draperies in each of these rooms had been pulled back allowing the dramatic afternoon sunlight to enter unimpeded. George, seemingly unwilling to put Isabel down, carried her through every room as she exclaimed, "Oh, how perfectly beautiful!"

Isabel could see at once that the entire place had been decorated by a professional interior designer who had used shades of soft blue and green, essentially bringing inside the colors of the water and making the Gulf of Mexico a "fourth wall." Ivory upholstery and elegant material of blue and gold stripes alternated with seafoam green silk. Each room had some element of chinoiserie from the silk screen over the sofa depicting some herons, to Asian lamps of blue and white porcelain, to a blue, cream and pink Chinese wallpaper in the master bedroom.

George deposited Isabel on the bed and when she started to raise herself up on her elbows, he gently pushed her back down and began kissing her insistently on the lips. His mouth went from her face to her neck, and he began unbuttoning her blouse and softly caressing her breasts. Isabel instantly understood that their "wedding night" would take place in the afternoon before they had even unpacked, and she briefly regretted that her lovely, new white lace nightgown was in the bottom of a suitcase. She knew herself well enough to realize that this trivial detail was in her thoughts because she did not want to face the facts that truly concerned her. When she agreed to marry him, Isabel had told George that she was still a virgin, and he had not pressed her further. Knowing instinctively that he would be patient with her, she was not afraid of the physical pain she might suffer. What she feared was far more subtle. If George saw sex as something approaching a sacred act between a husband and wife, if he elevated it to too high a plane, she knew she would be unable to achieve the feelings he might expect of her. Isabel hoped she would be able to respond physically, she thought her body might be able to reach orgasm, but she was very concerned about succeeding emotionally. She knew she could not reach ecstatic sexual heights through sheer force of will, and the idea of faking it either physically or emotionally was repugnant to her.

As George's hand moved along her inner thighs, Isabel began to desire him in a way she had not expected and she relaxed her body, allowing herself to enjoy these strange, new physical sensations. She tensed momentarily and made a small cry as she surrendered her virginity. George whispered, "Do you want me to stop?"

Isabel was grateful for his concern, but she felt the pain was bearable, and she bit her lip to prevent any more sounds escaping from her after she answered, "No, it's okay."

Later, as they lay side by side, George said, "I'm sorry I hurt you."

Isabel replied, "No, it was fine, really." She meant what she said. She had felt physical desire if not emotional passion, and she hoped that her worries might be groundless. This original impression was confirmed during the rest of their honeymoon. To her surprise, George treated sex as something primarily physical, natural and fun. As she grew to know him intimately, she realized that it sometimes served as a remedy for the stress and tensions in his work. She was relieved that he expected no more from her than she was able to give.

George and Isabel showered and changed, and he took her to a restaurant that Moira and John had recommended near St. Armand's Circle. For dinner they ordered lobster bisque and fried oysters and drank an excellent bottle of chardonnay. They ate leisurely, laughing and talking much of the time. Their silences were comfortable; they were at ease with each other.

Isabel lay awake that first night listening to the soft breathing of George sleeping beside her and the continuous pounding of the surf. She was content. She was now fully a wife, and she very much wanted to make her husband happy and, if possible, to make him proud of her.

The next morning, while George went to buy provisions for breakfast, Isabel walked out to the balcony and sat in a chair that had a direct view of the Gulf of Mexico. It was early still and the beach was largely deserted. A few people were walking briskly, and one or two others were sauntering, stopping periodically to examine seashells. Overhead gulls were crying, pelicans were gliding on the wind currents and sandpipers kept up their busy dance at the edge of the waves. The sun, still on the eastern side of the building, shone on the water, and Isabel was intrigued by the beauty of the fluid colors: deep blue in the distance, teal nearer shore and, finally, pale green as the waves broke continuously with their shifting borders of white foam.

Isabel wondered what it would be like to own this condominium. She had always believed that her grandparent's property, their house and land, the house with the grandeur of its Georgian symmetry and the lawns and flower beds sweeping down to the river, had to be the most beautiful place in the world to live. But she could see how one could easily become mesmerized by the sound of the surf and by this expanse of water which stretched endlessly to the horizon, interrupted only occasionally by a distant sailboat.

In thinking about her grandparent's home, Isabel knew that its intrinsic beauty was not solely responsible for its hold on her. Because many of her earliest memories were formed there, she understood that part of her fascination lay in the fact that those memories were fragments of a time when most of her life lay before her and everything seemed possible. Now that she was older, now that she was married, she had reached a point where her past was as much a part of her as her future. She wondered how she would feel today if her mother were still alive. What would have happened if she had never met Jean-Marc? Was she destined never to love George with the same intensity and passion she had felt for him? These were dangerous thoughts; Isabel knew they were leading her in the wrong direction and to a place she did not wish to go.

As she stood up and grasped the railing, a gust of wind blew her hair into her eyes. She brushed it away with her hand and concerned herself with other people's lives and other people's difficulties. If Emily Dickinson had lived when there was therapy available for her inordinate shyness, if Virginia Woolf, existing on the edge of madness, had been given access to antidepressants, if T. S. Eliot's first marriage had been happy, would the world now enjoy their works? She was curious to know how much of what they produced was influenced by their emotional pain.

George called out from the hall, "I'm back!" and Isabel went in to find him holding a paper bag filled with freshly baked croissants, a carton of orange juice, a pound of expensive coffee and copies of the *New York Times* and the *Longboat Observer*. The latter contained an article about a nearby farm where white Lipizzaner stallions were sheltered and trained. Isabel put the croissants in the microwave and began to read about the horses.

"Darling," she said, "this is fascinating. Did you know that the stallions aren't born white – they turn white gradually as they grow? The manes and tails are the last things to turn. Oh, it says here that the public is allowed to visit the farm two days a week!" Looking up, she saw George smiling at her and removing the croissants from the oven. She had failed to hear the beep the oven made when the time was up.

"I think I know someone who just might like to go to that farm," George remarked.

"Oh, yes, I'd love to!" Isabel exclaimed.

Isabel's first test came when she saw the parsonage allocated to the newly married associate pastor. It was euphemistically dubbed a "Victorian cottage." Time, however, had stolen its original gingerbread and its ornate casements. All that was left was a hulking shell with peeling white shingles, serviceable large plate-glass windows, and an interior inexplicably painted throughout in an anemic pink. Former occupants had left a mission-style dining room set and a wooden-framed sofa upholstered in huge yellow flowers on brown vines. On the living room wall was a large still life with a black background, the better to emphasize the vase of bright and enormous blooms that Isabel thought had a sort of voracious, fly-trap quality about them.

The church had formed a committee of ladies to assist Isabel in decisions about the renovation and decorating of the property. Two of the women were from the Smithers family, and George had told her that this family was a weighty one where the parish was concerned. They also contributed generously to church funds each year. Miss Agatha Smithers, a tall, slender, grey-haired woman could only be described as elegant. She wore black and lavender almost exclusively, with a double strand of pearls always at her throat. She was joined on the committee by her sister-in-law, Mrs. J. Addison Smithers. Mrs. Smithers, in her mid-fifties, Isabel guessed, was a stout woman with a large bosom. She had small, rather vacant hazel eyes, and her dyed blonde hair was done in a style of tight ringlets that bounced when she moved. She and her husband had recently returned to Connecticut after living for a decade in Honolulu. The islands, it seemed, were still very much in their blood. They affected large, colorful Hawaiian print muu muus and matching Aloha shirts.

Mrs. Smithers invariably arrived at church just before the service was to begin in order to bestow the largesse of her greetings on people on both sides of the aisle as she walked to her pew at the front. Mr. J. Addison always followed a few paces behind her, his head bent down staring at the floor. Isabel had the distinct impression that he hoped, in some vague way, that people would not associate him with his wife. Isabel trusted he was not aware that some of the parishioners referred to the pair as "the Jaddisons."

At the first meeting of the decorating committee, Mrs. Smithers came with a portfolio full of suggestions.

"My dear," she said, beaming at Isabel, her blonde curls dancing, "I think I can help you have a really distinctive house. You know you will be doing quite a bit of entertaining for the church, and you will certainly need a lot of new things. Instead of a sideboard in the dining room, we could build you an inexpensive thatched tiki bar where you could put dishes for buffets. And I've brought some wonderful, bright Hawaiian fabrics back with me. There is enough material to make several pairs of curtains. Then, don't you think basic brown would be a lovely color for all of the interior walls? I mean, it's just so neutral; it goes with everything. And outside, you could extend the tropical theme by putting some tiki torches around the terrace and..."

Isabel's heart was sinking, and she was in a dilemma about how she could nullify these, to her way of thinking, totally inappropriate ideas. She decided to enter the fray while keeping her voice subdued and resolutely pleasant.

"I think it might be very nice to have brown somewhere," she said. "Perhaps we could use it in my husband's study. But the tiki bar idea troubles me a bit because I have seen such things used in the décor of seafood restaurants as places to have cocktails, and we would certainly want to avoid any such reference in a parsonage, wouldn't we?" She smiled sweetly at Mrs. J. Addison who frowned and said, "I never meant ..."

Suddenly, there was a strong, confident voice from the

opposite side of the table. Miss Smithers was speaking.

"Eleanor," she said, interrupting her sister-in-law, "I think you have forgotten that we are in Connecticut. Trying to make a Victorian cottage into some tropical hut is absurd. I'm sure the rest of the committee will agree with me on that. If you like, we can vote."

But Eleanor Smithers knew when she was beaten. She was, after all, a Smithers only by marriage, and Miss Smithers controlled the largest share of the family's fortune.

"No," she said. "No, of course, Agatha. I do see what you mean."

Isabel heaved an inward sigh of relief and managed to smile at Miss Smithers in a way that she hoped would sufficiently convey her gratitude.

Miss Smithers gave Isabel a small nod and continued. "This is to be the Larsson's home as well as a parsonage, and I suggest, Mrs. Larsson, that you and your husband draw up a list of colors you would like. One of the church's parishioners who is a contractor has offered to paint the house inside and out and make any necessary repairs at a greatly reduced rate. I think this committee will also want to give you a small stipend toward some new furniture."

Isabel smiled and replied, "Thank you very much."

Isabel met George after the committee meeting, and they started to walk back to the parsonage.

"How did it go?" he said, chuckling when Isabel explained what had transpired. She, however, failed to see the humor in the situation.

"It wasn't funny, George! You told me the Smithers are important to the church – and here I was taking the chance of offending one of them!"

"Sorry, darling. But actually, I'm very proud of you.

You handled the situation just as you should have. Try to cultivate Agatha Smithers; she has a very sensible head on her shoulders. As for Mrs. J. Addison, well, let's just say that she is, perhaps, not quite as clear headed. She has a thing for brown and beige. A couple of months ago, she headed the committee to paint my office at the church. I couldn't have cared less what color they picked, but as I recall, the color chosen was called "Big on Beige." And, oh yes, a small crèche she donated to the rummage sale was totally beige as well; I've never seen one like it before or since."

"Good heavens!" Isabel exclaimed.

"What I'm trying to say here is to choose your battles carefully. Defend what you truly care about; give in gracefully if you feel neutral or nearly neutral about a subject. And, by the way, welcome to the world of church politics!"

"Just what sort of a rejoinder do you expect me to make to that remark?" Isabel asked as she looked at George and grimaced.

"In celebration, let's go home and hit the sherry?" George replied.

Three days later, Isabel met with Mr. Grant, the contractor. He was a large, balding, affable man who presented a paint chart of possible colors. In consultation with George, Isabel decided on a pale blue for the exterior, and, bound by the word "necessary" as far as improvements, she dipped into her own inheritance from her mother to buy some Victorian trim which, when painted white, contrasted nicely with the fresh blue.

She saw at once that the interior would have to be eclectic. There were no funds to attempt any particular period. She stripped the mahogany stain from the furniture leaving the original light wood which she covered with a clear coat of varnish. The yellow flowers on the sofa, with their brown vines, were replaced by a soft green check. She extended the use of pale green and other pastels on the walls in all of the rooms. Searching local flea markets, she found pieces with potential and, with George's help, she attended estate auctions, bidding for bargains they could cart home in the back of their station wagon. Splurging on a green and white toile duvet with matching curtains for the master bedroom was her only extravagance, and when the house was finished, parishioners and guests commented on her excellent taste. Isabel had an innate ability to sense what furnishings would be aesthetically pleasing and respectable for a parsonage without ever crossing the line to pretensions that might jar or provoke envy.

 George liked to do counseling in his study that was just to the left off the foyer as people came through the front door. Isabel had made the room very welcoming with a soothing blend of various shades of beige and cream. There was a large bookcase filled with books including George's few, prized first editions, his collection of small marble elephants and framed family photographs. Two comfortable, overstuffed chairs flanked a fireplace where George used even the slightest chill in the air as an excuse to light a fire. There were fresh flowers in pastel vases on tables around the room; these came from the garden in summer and from the greenhouse, shared with the senior pastor at the manse, in winter. Often, if a counseling session lasted for more than the usual time, Isabel would rap at the door, carrying a tray of tea and home-baked cookies.

 The length of counseling sessions varied. Some were so short that Isabel barely had time to think about serving tea. Sessions with engaged couples, who thought their

WHILE THE MUSIC LASTS

love, undoubtedly, would carry them through anything the world had to hurl at them, tended to be brief. Bereavement counseling often took longer, and George told Isabel he had determined that, on average, it usually took a year and a half for someone to recover from the loss of a spouse.

Rarely, Isabel approached the study door carrying a tray and realized that her interruption would be unwelcome and inappropriate. One such time occurred when George was counseling a seventeen-year-old girl whose twelve-year-old brother had just died of leukemia. Isabel heard the girl say, "The nurse called my mother. She said, 'Oh, Mrs. Nelson, he's going! He's going!' and my mother ran and knelt by the bed and cried my brother's name over and over saying, 'Larry, Larry, Larry!'"

Isabel heard silence and then the beginning of the girl's sobbing. She quietly turned and retraced her steps to the kitchen. Later, when the girl emerged red-eyed from the study, Isabel helped her on with her coat and wordlessly gave her a hug before sending her out into the cold, dark February afternoon. Snow had been forecast all that day and the first flakes were beginning to fall.

Isabel entered happily into the life of the parish. She helped with children's Bible classes, held women's circle meetings, for which she often baked cakes and pastries, and gave private piano lessons to a growing number of young students.

When she had been married six months, Isabel realized her period was late and that she had absolutely no appetite for breakfast. Occasionally she felt nauseated in the early morning. She and George were eager to start a family, and she wanted to spare him false hope, so she secretly made an appointment with the gynecologist. She need not have worried because the test showed a positive result. Isabel felt overjoyed and immediately wanted to share the news with George. She stood looking out of the living-room window watching impatiently for him to come up the walk. When she saw him, she went to the door and flung it wide. She was beaming as George came in, and she took him by the hand and led him to the sofa. She sat down and patted the cushion to indicate that he should sit beside her.

"Darling," she said, " you are going to be a father!"

George repeated, "A father…" and then, as the full import of her words struck him, he turned white and seemed dumbstruck. Finally he stammered out, "Oh, dear Lord, how marvelous! Are you sure?"

"The test came out positive," Isabel replied, and she and George dissolved into happy, excited laughter. That evening they started the search for names for a boy or girl and discussed the logistics of turning the spare room into a nursery.

Isabel had just passed her first trimester when she was awakened from a deep sleep by a cramping pain in her lower abdomen. As she sat up, she felt a gushing wetness between her legs. She turned on the light, thrust back the covers and looked in horror at the bright red blood staining her nightgown and the sheet beneath her.

"Oh, no," she moaned, "no, no, no!"

George woke immediately saying, "Darling?" and then as he saw the ever- increasing amount of blood, "Oh, my God, we have to get you to the hospital!"

The gynecologist was sympathetic as she explained that Isabel had suffered what is known as "an inevitable miscarriage." Nothing Isabel or George could have done would have changed the outcome. Sometimes, she explained, the placenta separates from the wall of the uterus. Often, miscarriages occur when the fetus has a developmental abnormality. "It's nature's way of stopping something that just isn't right," she said.

"How long do I have to wait until we can try again?" Isabel asked.

"We like you to give your body time to recover, to wait until you have had at least one normal period."

"But I will be able to get pregnant again? This doesn't mean I won't get pregnant again, does it?"

"I see no reason why you should have trouble conceiving," the doctor reassured them.

When Isabel arrived home again, she suddenly burst into great, heaving sobs. Nothing George said seemed to make any difference, and once he had exhausted all of the logical arguments, he decided simply to hold her until she stopped crying.

Two weeks passed and Isabel seemed to be making little headway against her lethargy and depression. George suggested that she might benefit from some short-term counseling, and Isabel agreed. Isabel told her therapist that she was astounded by the depth of her grief.

"I just feel completely devastated. I don't want to get out of bed in the morning."

"Your gynecologist has told you that you can still have children, so why do you think you feel such overwhelming grief?"

Isabel hesitated. Finally she said, "I have been thinking about my mother a lot. I lost her suddenly when I was seventeen. This grief almost seems to be tied to her loss in some way. I can't explain the connection but I know it's there. And I wanted the baby so much. You see, I thought of it as my baby from the moment I knew I was pregnant. So I just feel like a failure as a woman. It's irrational, I know, but that's how I feel."

"Do you think you could be grieving for something else in addition to losing your mother and the baby?"

"I don't know what you mean."

"You mentioned that your grief may be disproportionate. Could there be something more that is making you sad?"

"I don't think so. I'm really fortunate in my life right now."

Gradually, Isabel worked through her emotional distress and was helped unexpectedly when Mrs. Wilde, the organist and choir director, announced that her husband had accepted a job in another state and that she would be leaving. Isabel applied for the position and, with her excellent qualifications, was the obvious choice of the committee. Being able to immerse herself in music once again kept Isabel in good spirits, and in addition, she volunteered one day a week at the local Humane Society. During her first month there, she brought home a scrawny white kitten and called her Blanche, telling George she chose the name from the Tennessee Williams' character in *A Streetcar Named Desire* who, insane and lost, commented that she had "always depended on the kindness of strangers."

After Isabel brought home a puppy, an older stray dog and another kitten, George took her aside and said, "Darling, this is really enough. I know you mean well, but we simply can't take in any more needy animals."

He had little patience with housebreaking the puppy and was very disturbed by "accidents."

Isabel was at a loss at this turn of events. She could not bear to see adorable animals at the shelter undergo euthanasia when she was sure there would be many more adoptions than there were currently, if only people knew about them. How could she make people aware?

George vetoed her idea of putting pictures in the church bulletin on Sundays telling her that was undoubtedly the wrong venue. It was then that Isabel decided to go to the nearest local television station. She armed herself with photographs of kittens and puppies, asked to speak to the manager, explained who she was and essentially begged him for five minutes of airtime a week to showcase animals who needed homes. Isabel could be very persuasive, and the manager, who had pets of his own, recognized that he could air shelter tapes as part of the station's community service programming. Isabel could hardly wait to get home to inform George of her success.

It was at the time that Isabel was continually cleaning up after the puppy she had rescued that she began to realize George had something of a revulsion concerning bodily functions, animal or human. At the time of her miscarriage, he had insisted that they throw away the bedding that had been soiled rather than attempting to clean it. One summer night, she had eaten some chicken salad in a restaurant. Later, she discovered that the dish must have been out of the refrigerator too long, because she was violently ill with vomiting and diarrhea. George was repulsed and could not bear to be near her. He took his pillow and a blanket and went into the guest room.

Isabel noticed that George was more than willing to perform all of his duties as pastor with the exception of having to visit the sick in the hospital. She had to prod him to go and, finally, understanding how difficult this part of his work was for him, she decided to help by accompanying him. Isabel was comfortable around the ill, and she would unobtrusively put herself forward, taking their hands and putting her head near to hear what they said, thus allowing George to stay more in the background.

WHILE THE MUSIC LASTS

At this time, Isabel noticed that there were hospital volunteers, women and teenaged girls known as "candy stripers" because they wore pink and white smocks. The idea of helping in this way appealed to her. When she brought the subject up, George, thinking of his own aversion, was amazed that anyone would willingly put herself in such a position, but after he thought about it, he realized that Isabel's natural empathy would serve her well in such an undertaking. She applied to be a volunteer and was placed in the pediatric ward.

All went well for several months. Isabel enjoyed reading to the children, talking with them and playing easy games. She often became so engrossed in what she was doing that her shift was over before she realized it.

She found the children, for the most part, incredibly resilient and stoical. There were times when she would come to the hospital and discover an empty bed where a terminally ill child she knew had died. This was very hard on her, but she never considered leaving until one day when she was asked to go read to a child who was mildly retarded and was recovering from surgery to straighten a curvature of the spine.

She chose some simple books and went down the corridor to his room. When she entered, he was lying on his side in the bed and moaning. She tried to speak to him, but he began to cry out in pain, saying, "Oh, please, please help me!"

The idea of reading to him was ludicrous. He was obviously in agony. Isabel ran to the station where the nurses on duty were laughing and talking with each other.

"The boy in room 212 is in horrible pain," Isabel said. "Please, you have to do something!"

The nurses were irritatingly nonchalant as they

explained that only the doctor could prescribe more drugs for pain. They were giving the boy all the medication the doctor had ordered.

"Well," Isabel said, "get in touch with the doctor, then, and explain that it's not enough."

"We can't do that," they said.

When Isabel insisted, they just stood and looked at her. She felt a mixture of exasperation and sorrow. There was nothing she could do. Finally, she put the books she was carrying down on the counter of the nurses' station and walked out with tears running down her cheeks.

She was still utterly dejected when George arrived home for dinner, and she had to apologize for the fact that she had given the meal no thought at all.

"I'll order some pizza," he said.

"It was just horrible to see that boy in such pain, and the nurses didn't seem to care at all!"

"I'm sure they did care but they probably have to distance themselves somewhat from patients. They can't allow themselves to become too emotional; with all of the situations they encounter, they'd never get their work done."

Isabel seemed unconvinced. "You weren't there, George. They didn't care."

"Well, if something like this is going to affect you to this extent, then I think you might give some thought to ending your work as a volunteer. I could never understand how you had the stomach for it in the first place."

Isabel was trying to decide what to do when the matter was taken out of her hands. She discovered she was once again pregnant, and since she had miscarried previously, her gynecologist told her to cut back on all non-essential work and rest in bed as much as possible.

WHILE THE MUSIC LASTS

Isabel was determined to be successful in her second pregnancy. She followed her doctor's instructions to the letter, carefully watching her weight, eating only wholesome foods, foregoing her favorite ice creams and chocolates, and when, eventually, she was permitted some gentle exercise, she began walking conscientiously thirty minutes each day.

When an ultrasound determined that Isabel would have a little girl, she enlisted George's help in turning the spare room into a nursery. He painted the walls a delicate shade of pink and Isabel stenciled little fluffy lambs as a border. She found some relatively inexpensive white, ruffled voile curtains that she used at the windows and to trim around the edge of the bassinet. She then incorporated small blue accents throughout the room.

One of the women in the parish gave a baby shower for her, and Isabel received little pink outfits, crib blankets, stuffed animals, a silver cup and a long-handled baby spoon. She was given several children's books including a complete A. A. Milne which contained *When We Were Very Young, Now We Are Six* and all of the Pooh stories. Isabel's mother had read these to her when she was small, and Isabel was eager to share them with her own daughter whose name, she and George had finally decided, would be Emily.

Isabel suffered morning sickness at the beginning of her pregnancy, and she developed the habit of turning up the volume of the clock radio as soon as it came on in the morning. She would then run to the bathroom, making sure to close the door behind her, to keep the sound of her gagging from George. She was certain he knew she was being considerate and was grateful, although he never said anything to her about it.

WHILE THE MUSIC LASTS

Isabel wanted to deliver naturally but was not at all sure how to introduce the subject of childbirth classes to George. She wanted to learn breathing and relaxation exercises and hoped George would be her coach, but she doubted he would be willing to become that involved. She was aware that he would have been far happier in Victorian days when, after a confinement, the husband was simply presented with a child, having had very little or nothing to do with the actual birth process.

Isabel sent off for some literature and took several books out of the library. She then decided to leave them lying about in conspicuous places. George did take the hint, eventually, and one evening he said, "I see you are considering natural childbirth."

"Yes," Isabel answered.

"And you want me to become involved in this?"

Isabel hesitated. "I would very much like to have you as my coach, if you think you can bear it."

George was silent for a moment and then said, "It isn't really about whether I can bear it. It's about you - about you being able to take the pain. I know now that I won't be able to stand seeing you suffer. If you promise me that you will ask for relief - for - what do they call it?

"An epidural," Isabel replied.

"If you will accept that if you need it and not try to tough it out, no matter what, then I will do my best to help you."

Isabel agreed immediately. The question of whether or not he would be present in the delivery room during the actual birth was yet to be determined, but Isabel decided she would leave that until later and savor the victory she had achieved.

WHILE THE MUSIC LASTS

A few days before her due date, Isabel felt that she should clean the entire house in preparation for the new baby. She dusted and vacuumed, scrubbed and polished, and that night, at two in the morning, she went into labor.

George drove her to the hospital and, after looking both ways to be sure no one was coming, went through a red light deliberately. He smiled to himself, thinking, if a policeman stopped him, he would explain the situation, and the policeman would say, "Follow me!" and lead them to the hospital with lights flashing and siren blaring. Nothing so dramatic occurred, however.

A wheelchair was brought for Isabel as she checked in. She and George then went up to the maternity ward together. True to her word, Isabel accepted a shot of Demerol as her contractions intensified. She could still feel the pain but was able to breathe through it without complaining. The main effect of the drug was to allow her to relax and sleep between contractions.

George sat beside her through the night and into the early morning. After hours of waking and doing breathing exercises with George's encouragement, then falling asleep again, Isabel was pleased to find the pain, though it was steadily increasing, was not so severe that she had to groan or cry out.

She wanted to remain silent for two reasons. First, she had no intention of asking for an epidural, and she had to keep George calm, especially if she hoped to have him beside her during the delivery. The other reason was more capricious and went back to her childhood antipathy to making a scene in public. When she was young, if something upset her, she waited to cry until she was safely in her own home, and she still had a certain pride in being able to remain stoical. Emotional pain had broken her once. She was determined not to allow physical pain to do the same.

The obstetrician told her that her cervix was fully effaced and that she could start to push whenever she wished. By this time, Isabel was feeling exhausted and thought she would wait awhile to push. But a pain suddenly struck her unlike any she had felt before. Her entire body seemed to be involved, and the force of the contraction caused her to sit up and gasp. This, she thought, must be the second stage of labor. If pushing would help, then Isabel was definitely ready to try. When the next contraction began, Isabel bore down with everything she had and found that, while she was pushing hard, the pain subsided. Her body was showing her what she needed to do.

The nurse told Isabel to look in the mirror near her feet and the doctor said, "You can see the baby's head emerging." He took her hand and placed it, so that she could actually feel the top of the head.

At this point, George slumped into a chair then slid to the floor. He had fainted. The nurses laid him on his back, patted his cheeks and fanned him with some papers. He began to revive just as Emily was born and gave her first, strong healthy cry.

Isabel smiled. George struggled to his feet and went to see mother and baby. Emily was lying on Isabel's stomach.

"She's beautiful," George said and then, somewhat sheepishly, "I'm sorry about…"

Isabel cut him off. "Don't worry," she said. "We're all fine now. That's what matters."

She had warned the doctor previously not to suggest that George might want to cut the cord. She knew he would want nothing to do with such a procedure.

From the start, Emily was an easy baby. She was soon sleeping through the night, and Isabel was nursing her successfully. The beautiful, helpless child at her breast generated waves of solicitude and tenderness in Isabel. She adored this amazing little creature with the soft tufts of strawberry blonde hair, hair that looked as if an artist had happily blended Isabel's red with George's white blonde. She marveled at her daughter's incredibly blue eyes and tiny, perfectly formed hands and feet. It was apparent that her features resembled those of her father, which meant, Isabel hoped, that she would grow up to look like Alice.

Alice, in fact, took two weeks off from work and came to help Isabel as soon as she and Emily were home from the hospital. When Alice held Emily, Isabel thought that the family resemblance was uncanny. People could easily mistake Alice for Emily's mother.

Unlike George, Alice was ready to take on just about anything. She willingly changed soiled diapers, something her brother managed to avoid. When Emily, in her little portable baby seat, would start to turn red and grunt at the dinner table, Alice would rise immediately and take her to the changing table to remove her quickly from George's view. She brought clean towels when Emily spit up. She did laundries, cooked and washed dishes and allowed Isabel to get some much-needed rest.

One evening, when Emily and George were both in bed, Isabel asked Alice about George's reluctance to have anything to do with diapers or messes in general.

Alice hesitated. Finally she said, "I think George should tell you this himself; but since he hasn't, you may as well know the truth. George wet the bed for quite a long time when he was a boy. The bad thing about it was that my father spanked him for it. Our father is not a cruel man, and he never raised his hand to us otherwise, but for some reason, he saw bed-wetting as a moral failure, and he responded in what we now know was probably the worst way. So George developed this phobia, and I suppose he is just too embarrassed to say anything to you about it."

Isabel's heart immediately went out to George and she said, "Oh, I'm so sorry!"

Emily's pediatrician had asked Isabel to check in with him at periodic intervals, and soon he told her to introduce infant cereal mixed in some warm two-percent milk. Isabel held Emily and tried to feed her the pablum with a long-handled baby spoon. Emily rejected each spoonful by pushing it around with her tongue until most of the cereal was in a circle around the outside of her mouth. Isabel would scrape it off and begin again with the same result. After nearly forty-five minutes of this, Isabel was almost ready to cry from frustration. Once again, Alice came to the rescue.

"You know," she said, "Emily suckles wonderfully. Obviously she doesn't quite understand how to deal with solid food. How would it be to get a baby bottle, enlarge the nipple so you could put both the milk and cereal in and see if she will take it that way?"

The suggestion was an immediate success. Emily happily accepted her bottles of warm milk and pablum. She was growing rapidly and giving her first smiles to everyone around her.

When it was time for Alice to leave, Isabel gave her a hug and said, "I can't thank you enough! I'm so sorry to see you go, and its not just because of all you have done but because I'll really miss your company. Please visit us often."

"Oh, you won't be able to get rid of me," Alice laughed. "I love being an aunt." She picked up Emily and cradled her gently in her arms then kissed her softly on the forehead before handing her to Isabel.

Shortly before Emily was born, Isabel hung the painting of the woman in the Venetian gondola in her nursery. She had every intention of "going into the picture" with her daughter just as her mother had with her. When Emily began to notice things around her and pointed at the painting, Isabel would say, "Yes, a pretty lady in a boat! See the boat! See the water!" Eventually, Emily's first word was "boat." Her pronunciation may have lacked the final "t," and the word sounded more like "bow," but both George and Isabel, who were present when this first attempt was made, had no doubt that their daughter was referring to the gondola.

Isabel inherited her grandparents' house. She could not bear to put it up for sale, although George advised that was the best course of action. She pointed out to him that, since they lived in a parsonage, the family home was the only one they actually owned. Secretly, she hoped to retire there one day. In the meantime, her father was nearing retirement and was once again debating whether or not to leave his apartment in the city. After talking it over with George, Isabel decided to offer him her grandparents' house when he stopped working. It had been her mother's home until she married, and Isabel thought he might enjoy living in the place that had meant so much to his wife. Her father was deeply touched by the offer and accepted almost at once.

Any concerns Isabel had about her father living in the house alone were alleviated by the fact that Andrew had an extra key and would look in on him occasionally. Andrew had finished law school at Cornell and was using his old room next door while he was establishing himself in his father's law practice in town.

"It's good of you to keep an eye on Dad," Isabel said.

"He may be retired, but he's certainly still very vigorous," Andrew replied. "I'm sure there won't be any problems. Since he's there alone, though, it might not be a bad idea to have an alarm system installed. The alarms aren't just for burglars; they have special buttons to push – panic buttons – if anything at all is wrong… if he should suddenly become ill…"

"Yes," Isabel said, "I agree. That's an excellent suggestion."

"I'm just so glad you decided not to sell the house. It would seem so odd to have strangers living there after all these years."

Isabel, George and Emily visited as often as they could, and Andrew watched as Emily grew to be an astonishingly beautiful eight-year-old. One summer day when George, Isabel, Andrew and Emily were sitting out in the garden, Emily followed Blanche, the cat, who was getting on in years, into the grape arbor. Andrew took the opportunity to say that he was certain that, if they wanted, George and Isabel could get Emily into print or television commercials.

"One of my good friends at Cornell went into entertainment law," he said. "He's in New York City now, and he has connections. Emily is absolutely gorgeous. She could probably make enough money to pay for her college education and then some."

George immediately demurred. "Thank you for saying that, Andrew. We're very flattered, but Emily's great grandparents established a trust for her education, and I think having her go for auditions… The children do have to audition, don't they?"

"Yes," Andrew replied, "they do."

"Well, I think that could be a bit rough on her, especially if she should be rejected."

"But, I'm sure she wouldn't be," Andrew replied.

"Still, there are no guarantees, are there? I don't think we would want to take that chance."

Isabel smiled at Andrew. "Thanks anyway," she said. "It's dear of you to think of her in that way."

Later she would confide her real concern to Andrew. She was certain George feared that the church might think Emily was being exploited if she acted in commercials and was paid for it.

Two months later, Isabel received a letter from Andrew.

"I'm sure you have just about given up on me and decided I'll always be a confirmed old bachelor, haven't you? Well, surprise! I've met a woman named Amanda Jenkins, and we've decided to get married in six months. I can't wait to have her meet you. You'll like her. She teaches English at SUNY, Binghamton. We're buying the small house four doors down from my parents, number 490 Front Street. Do you remember it? So, if your father is away sometimes, I'll still be able to watch your house. And, oh, by the way, we'd like to borrow Emily to be the flower girl at our wedding. We don't have any relatives the right age (or any as beautiful for that matter!) Of course, you and George are invited as well. (Formal invitation will follow closer to the date.) Love always, Andrew"

Isabel wrote back immediately, saying how happy she was, and agreeing that Emily could be the flower girl.

The day of the wedding, in early September, was perfect, with temperatures in the seventies and a clear blue sky. As Andrew had predicted, Isabel did like Amanda. She was a petite brunette with warm brown eyes and a ready smile. She and Andrew were married in the conservatory of his parents' house. Chairs had been brought in with space left for an aisle that was lined at intervals with bouquets of white roses. There were additional flowers in front of the window where the minister stood while Andrew and Amanda said their vows.

Emily, delighted with her flower girl's dress of ivory silk trimmed with lace and with a blue satin sash to go around her waist, performed impeccably, her reddish blonde curls shone as she scattered pink rose petals before the bride.

The reception was held in a large white tent in the back garden. Isabel knew most of the guests and introduced them to George and Emily. After the bride's bouquet was tossed and the last dance, there were joyful hugs all around as the newlyweds prepared to leave to drive to New York City. They were embarking on their honeymoon, a cruise to Bermuda, the next day.

PART FOUR

You who never arrived

in my arms, Beloved, who were lost

from the start,

I don't even know what songs

would please you. I have given up trying

to recognize you in the surging wave of the next

moment. All the immense

images in me – the far-off, deeply-felt landscape,

cities, towers, and bridges, and un-

suspected turns in the path,

and those powerful lands that were once

pulsing with the life of the gods -

all rise within me to mean

you, who forever elude me.

                        Rainer Maria Rilke

It had been a bad day and Isabel had difficulty falling asleep. Emily, on the verge of turning thirteen, was in a full-blown adolescent rebellion. She and a girlfriend had skipped an afternoon of school to go to a sale at the nearby mall.

As usual, George was no help when it came to discipline. Through the years of her marriage, Isabel had found that the equability of George's personality, the very blandness that originally relieved her of having to express a conjugal fervor that she did not feel, also had another side that was far less accommodating. Although George could be tenacious on his own, he disliked confrontation and his efforts to avoid it had repercussions both within and outside the family.

He could never bring himself to punish Emily verbally or even to set limits. All of this was left to Isabel, and the result was that, while Emily loved and respected her mother, she knew that she could manipulate her father.

To punish Emily's transgression, Isabel told her she would not be allowed to go to the movies with her friends on Saturday afternoon. This led to tears, a stomping upstairs and a loud slamming of Emily's bedroom door. George avoided the issue by retreating to his study.

For years, Isabel had managed this role of disciplinarian at home, but she was powerless to intervene effectively when George's weakness incurred problems for the church. Not long before, a parishioner who came reliably each Sunday morning and made generous contributions to church funds, took George aside and suggested that he swap some land of his own for land belonging to the church. George, without thinking the matter through, and eager only to please the gentleman, said he thought that would be a fine idea. The man in question left believing an agreement had been reached.

When the church's lawyer looked into the case, it was determined that the swap would be distinctly disadvantageous for the church. George's embarrassment was palpable, and he came to Isabel for advice. "I've made a mess of this situation," he said. "I'm not sure what to do next."

"Why not invite the man to come here to the parsonage some afternoon for tea? You can take him into your study and tell him how much his generosity to the church has meant through the years. Then tell him that you were too hasty in agreeing to his idea of a land swap because all such decisions have to be approved by the church's lawyer. Apologize to him for misleading him and hope he understands."

"But he may be terribly angry. He might even decide to leave the church."

"Yes, that's true. But I'm sorry, dear, I can't think of a better solution."

Isabel hoped that George might learn from the experience and be more cautious in the future, but she knew that was far from certain.

Emily was still sulking that evening when Isabel said good night. In bed, Isabel looked at the pattern on the ceiling formed by the windowpanes and the street lamp outside. Eventually, she slipped into her bathrobe and went down to the kitchen to warm a cup of milk.

She took her mug into the living room and curled up on the sofa. Clicking on the television, she was ready to watch any sort of mindless program and hoped for something boring that might make her sleepy. The hall clock had just chimed midnight when she switched to PBS. Charlie Rose was introducing his first guest.

Isabel, sipping her milk, reached into the drawer of the end table for a coaster.

"… the author of *Compassionate Care or Assisted Suicide?* Dr. Duncan Stewart. I am happy to have him at this table. Welcome."

"Thank you," Dr. Stewart replied with a smile. He was a man in his late forties or early fifties, thin, a little stooped with greying hair that he parted on the right and allowed to fall lankly on his high forehead. He had an oval face with slightly protruding ears, a strong chin and gentle, intelligent eyes.

"You are an oncologist which means that you deal with dying patients much of the time?" Charlie Rose began.

"Unfortunately, yes."

"And it is your contention that there would rarely be a need for assisted suicide if doctors made available to their patients all of the drugs that are out there to keep people comfortable in their final days?"

"Not only to make the drugs available, but to give them in sufficient doses. We have a history of under-treating pain in this country. This has not always been the fault of the physician. There are some draconian drug laws on the books which have made doctors frightened to prescribe enough medication."

"Frightened? You mean they think they might get in trouble with the law?"

"Precisely. They feel the Drug Enforcement Administration hovering over their shoulders. The agency recently created new guidelines saying that doctors who prescribe high dosages of opioids for chronic pain can be subject to criminal investigation. And there also seems to be a largely mythical fear of creating addiction in terminal patients."

"Would it matter?"

"I'm sorry, matter?"

"Yes, I mean if someone is dying, the most important thing would be to keep him or her comfortable, I should think. Would it matter if a terminally ill patient were addicted, since that patient was dying anyway?"

"Ah, there you get into a difficult philosophical question," Dr. Stewart replied. "Every physician takes the Hippocratic oath to 'first, do no harm.' The fact is, however, that it has been shown in various studies, that most patients are able to tolerate narcotics in sufficient doses to keep them comfortable without becoming addicted. I happen to believe that the risk of addiction is outweighed by the need for pain relief."

Dr. Stewart's manner lacked any stiffness or self-importance. It was apparent to Isabel that he cared deeply about his subject, and this made her want to hear more. She sat up and adjusted the volume a little higher.

"And you are concerned about pain relief generally, not only when people are terminally ill?"

"Yes, pain control for non-terminal patients could be much better than it is at present. Some of our beliefs are conditioned by our Judeo-Christian heritage. It used to be thought that women should suffer during childbirth because of the sin of Eve. Now enlightened people think that is arrant nonsense. But it takes time for old prejudices and biases to die."

Isabel vividly remembered the child who was recovering from spinal surgery.

"Yes!" she said softly to the television. "Just listen to the concern in his voice! This is not some pompous doctor who would treat you as if you were just a number or look at his watch fearing he would be late for his next golf game," she thought.

"We lag behind in this country," Dr. Stewart was saying. "For many years, England has used heroin and mixtures such as the so-called Brompton cocktail to keep terminal patients comfortable. We have been lax in teaching about pain control in our medical schools and even more remiss in failing to implement pain relief properly."

"Do you believe marijuana should be legalized for medicinal use?"

Dr. Stewart steepled his fingers which were long and very slender, almost delicate.

"Yes, there is data showing that marijuana can help restore the appetites of AIDS patients and cancer patients. If we disallow a substance because we are afraid of it, then the logical conclusion is that we should eliminate prescription drugs altogether. There are a lot of drugs out there, available only by prescription, which could cause horrific harm to people if given indiscriminately. Yet we are demonizing marijuana which, on a list of all prescription drugs, would be one of the more benign."

As Charlie Rose held up Dr. Stewart's book once again, Isabel found a pencil and jotted down the name. She would order it from the town's small, independent bookstore. The only thing she regretted about watching the program was that, once it was over, she was more awake than ever.

A month later, Isabel received a message on the answering machine from Ed Marsden, who was their family doctor, a parishioner and a friend. He asked her to call him back and to use the number at his clinic.

"Ed, it's Isabel Larsson. You wished to speak to me?"

"I'm sorry to bother you, but I think you might be able to help me with a problem."

"Yes? I hope so."

"I know you have done work with our county Humane Society. The thing is, Anna and I had to put our dog, Sandy, to sleep last week. She had cancer. She had been with us for nearly fifteen years and it was really rough on Anna. Since our youngest went off to college this fall, Anna was already suffering from what I think they call 'empty nest syndrome.' Then to lose the dog too..."

"Mmm, yes, I understand," Isabel murmured sympathetically.

"Well, I was hoping you might be able to help me find a puppy or a young dog who needs a home. Anna has been saying she wants to have you and George over for dinner - and I wonder if you would be willing to help me surprise her? I'd like to get a shelter dog and have you bring it with you the night you come to dinner. You could come in casually, for the evening and, a little later, go to your car and bring in the new dog. I know that would make her very happy, but it's asking a lot of you."

"What a lovely idea! I'd be delighted," Isabel said. "If you will meet me at the Humane Society one day next week, we can make the arrangements. There are always dogs who need to be adopted by good families."

"Yes, but I just hope I'm not putting you out too much."

"Not at all! I'm so pleased you thought of me."

"Would next Monday be all right with you - say around two?"

Isabel checked her calendar. "Fine," she said.

"Great - and Anna will be in touch with you about dinner."

When Isabel told George the plan, he was enthusiastic. "Anna Marsden has done so much volunteering for church suppers, it will be nice to be able to repay her a little. Just be sure that the only animal you rescue at the shelter is the dog for the Marsdens."

"I promise." Isabel smiled at him.

When Isabel arrived at the shelter promptly at two, Ed Marsden was already there waiting for her. They looked at several dogs, but Ed kept coming back to a two-year-old Golden Retriever who had recently had a litter of puppies. The puppies had been adopted, but the mother was available, and she was already housebroken. Her name was Sunshine.

The second time Ed came back to Sunshine and reached out to pet her, she licked his hand. The decision was made. "She's the one," he said.

Ed filled out the necessary paperwork, and Isabel explained that she would pick up Sunshine in five days. By then the dog would have been freshly bathed and have had an electronic identity chip implanted in her neck. The shelter would also supply the name of a veterinarian who would spay an adopted dog for a nominal fee.

"I have one more favor to ask," Ed said as they were leaving the shelter. There's an old friend of mine from college days coming to dinner with you and George. I was telling him about the two of you, and when I mentioned that you are a musician, he said he would love to hear you play. He's something of a musician himself – plays the violin. So I thought I'd ask you now rather than putting you on the spot later."

"I'd be happy to," Isabel smiled, "but I think I should have the right to ask that he bring along his violin. It's only fair that both of us play."

"It's a deal," Ed replied.

WHILE THE MUSIC LASTS

The afternoon of the dinner party, Isabel went to get Sunshine. She could understand why Ed had chosen her. Sunshine was not only a beautiful dog, but she had a certain dignity and serenity about her. Isabel had seen other shelter animals cower and tremble, often, she surmised, as the result of having been abused. But there was no trace of fear in Sunshine. She padded along confidently beside Isabel, and the ride home was uneventful. Since the day was warm and sunny, Isabel tied her under a tree in the yard and gave her some water. Before leaving for the shelter, she had made sure that her own dogs and cats were inside the house. There was no need to risk unnecessary confrontations.

Isabel put some old pillows and quilts in the back of the station wagon to use as a bed for Sunshine while she waited before being introduced to the Marsdens. She asked Emily to keep an eye on her while she went to dress.

When George came in the back door, Isabel had just finished showering.

"Hello," he called. "That is one great looking dog out there!"

"Yes, isn't she?" Isabel answered. "I think Anna will love her."

On the way to the Marsdens, Isabel suddenly thought of a logistical problem.

"George," she said, "I have agreed to play the piano after dinner, and another guest will be bringing his violin. That just will not be a good mix with a new dog coming into the house for the first time. Some dogs don't like live music; it hurts their ears and they can even howl. I was going to bring Sunshine in right after dessert – it would be easy to slip out while Anna is rinsing dishes. But now I think she shouldn't come in until after the music is over.

WHILE THE MUSIC LASTS

So what shall I do - finish playing and then make a mad dash for the front door? That will look ridiculous!"

George thought a few moments. "Obviously, that won't work. Tell you what: I'll sit close to the foyer while you play. When everything is just about to end, you give me a meaningful nod, and I'll slip out and get Sunshine and wait outside with her until the music stops."

"Perfect!" Isabel said. "Thanks, dear."

George parked the station wagon one half block away from the Marsden house. He and Isabel wanted to be sure Anna would not be able to see Sunshine too soon and spoil the surprise.

Ed and Anna welcomed them warmly. Ed took the drink orders in the form of a question. He had known them long enough to anticipate their preferences. " A single malt scotch for you, George, and a white wine for you, Isabel?"

George and Isabel said, "Yes, thanks," almost in unison.

"Isabel tells me we are to have the pleasure of meeting another couple tonight – friends of yours from college. And the husband plays the violin?" George asked.

"No, not a couple, just a college friend. He never married. He's…" Ed stopped and coughed. "Sorry, I have a tickle in my throat."

"Never married? Oh, I think I understand," George murmured.

"No, I'm probably giving you the wrong impression. He's not gay. He was deeply in love with a girl when we were in medical school, and he asked her to marry him but she turned him down. That episode hurt him so much that I think, for a long while, he was afraid to try again. Then he threw himself into medicine with a vengeance, and he still lives primarily for his work, I believe. He's an incredibly dedicated and gifted oncologist on staff at Yale's Grace-New Haven hospital."

"And he's a musician?" Isabel queried.

"Music is an avocation for him; he plays for the pure love of it. He and three other doctors have put together a chamber music quartet. They meet and play once a week, and, at least to my uneducated ear, they're really good. They perform each year at a benefit for the hospital. That will be coming up shortly, early next month, I think."

"There seems to be some connection between medicine and music or the sciences and music. I've known –" Isabel said, then stopped as the doorbell rang, and Anna rose to welcome her guest. Sounds of greeting came from the vestibule, and Anna reentered the living room followed by a slender, grey-haired man who appeared to be in his late forties to early fifties. As soon as Isabel saw him, she gave an audible gasp. Ed, Anna, and George turned to look at her.

Isabel felt herself blushing and was suddenly very shy. "I… I'm sorry." She stammered. "It's just that I feel know you," she said to the newcomer who, sensing that she was ill at ease, immediately sought to defuse the situation by introducing himself.

"Hello," he said, "I'm Duncan Stewart."

"Yes, I know," Isabel said, extending her hand. "I saw you on television."

Dr. Stewart shook her hand warmly. His eyes, which stared unwaveringly into hers, were at once both kind and gentle. He was not handsome in the customary sense of the word, but he had a presence that Isabel was sure inspired confidence in his patients.

Her response caused everyone to turn to her again. "I

saw you on the Charlie Rose show talking about your book on pain relief. I've just finished reading that book, and I think it's superb."

There was a collective sigh and some relieved laughter. Duncan Stewart smiled at Isabel. "Thank you for solving the mystery," he said. "When you said you knew me, I was reproaching myself for not recognizing you and wondering how on earth I could ever have forgotten you!" He immediately realized the implication of this response and reddened as Isabel blushed again.

Ed clapped Duncan Stewart heartily on the shoulder and said, "Come on in! I was just taking drink orders. Here, you can leave your violin on the piano bench. We are looking forward to hearing you both play after dinner."

"Oh, dear," Isabel said, shooting Dr. Stewart a glance of dismay.

"They're making us sing for our supper, aren't they?" he said, smiling at Isabel.

As they were finishing their soup, Isabel looked at Anna and said, "This is delicious. It's a pumpkin base, isn't it?"

"Yes, I'll be glad to give you the recipe if you like. I should warn you that we don't have it all that often because it's terrible for cholesterol. It has cheese, bacon and heavy cream in it."

"No wonder it's good!" George exclaimed. Turning to Duncan Stewart he asked, "Ed told us you work at Grace-New Haven. Do you live in New Haven as well?"

"Yes, although I'm a relative newcomer. I bought a studio condominium a few months ago that is close to the hospital. My family's home, where I grew up, was in New Canaan. I was sad to give it up, but after my mother died last year, my sister convinced me that, since property prices have risen astronomically recently, we should take advantage of the current market. She offered to go through everything and get the house ready to sell. That was the clincher. I'm a bit of a pack rat, so sorting and throwing away would take me forever."

"It's hard to part with things you've had a long time," Isabel murmured.

"Yes, and unfortunately my sister got rid of a few things I really wanted to keep."

Isabel looked up and saw Duncan Stewart staring at her intently. He hesitated, then said, "Forgive me for staring, it's just that you remind me…" He paused.

"Yes?" Isabel said.

"This may sound strange but – well, my mother was very fond of the works of the Pre-Raphaelites. We used to have a copy of Dante Gabriel Rossetti's painting of the *Blessed Damozel* above the fireplace in the dining room when I was a boy. You may know it. The woman has very red hair and is wearing some sort of loose green robe. Sitting there in your green dress, you remind me of that painting. I don't know whatever happened to it. I think my sister may have given it away or thrown it out which is too bad because I would have liked to have kept it."

"Yes, I know the painting and I'm flattered," Isabel smiled. She remembered lines from the Rossetti poem of the same name and said, softly,

> The blessed damozel leaned out
> From the gold bar of heaven;
> Her eyes were deeper than the depth
> Of waters stilled at even;

Dr. Stewart picked up the refrain:

> She had three lilies in her hand,
> And the stars in her hair were seven.

"That was one of my mother's favorite poems," he remarked.

Isabel said, "Rossetti wrote it as a sort of reverse of Poe's 'The Raven,' which most people know concerns the grief of a man for his dead love. Rossetti placed the *Blessed Damozel* in heaven yearning for her lover who is still alive on earth."

"I didn't know that about the relationship to Poe," Dr. Stewart said.

"Isabel loves poetry, don't you, dear?" George said, glancing fondly at his wife.

"I minored in English literature in college," Isabel replied almost apologetically. She was suddenly afraid that she sounded pedantic and was worried that she was boring everyone.

There was an awkward silence. Duncan Stewart broke it by commenting, "Debussy wrote a cantata on the *Blessed Damozel* called *La Damoiselle Elue*. Are you familiar with it? It's really beautiful."

"Yes!" Isabel said. "I have a very old and scratched recording of it. Once I tried to replace it, and I went into a music store at the mall that was blaring hard rock. A nice young boy, a teenager, waited on me. When I said *La Damoiselle Elue*, he asked me what language that was and how to spell it. He was very obliging and willing to help, but I think he thought I was from another planet!"

"Were you successful in getting it?" Anna asked.

"No, that hard rock should have warned me off! I'll have to try to get it on the net."

"I'm sure you can find it on Amazon," Ed said.

"Yes," Isabel said, and then, turning to Dr. Stewart, "I'm sorry you lost the picture. I know what it means when a painting has a long family history – and a sentimental value. We have a picture that I think my mother found at some garage sale originally. It's of a young woman sitting in a gondola in Venice. She has red hair. My daughter and I both have red hair, and that picture was used to calm us when we were little. If we were upset we pretended we could go into the picture and feel the gondola gently rocking and hear the gondolier sing. I can't imagine giving the painting up, even though I know it's not good art."

"Have you been to Venice – I mean in reality?" Duncan Stewart asked.

"No, my family and I were supposed to go the summer after I graduated from high school. But my mother died suddenly, and the trip had to be canceled."

The five of them were halfway through dinner before Anna brought up the subject of Sandy.

"You may be wondering why our dog wasn't here to give you her usual greeting. The thing is, we lost her ten days ago. Well, we didn't lose her in the sense that she ran away or anything, but she was quite sick with cancer, and we could tell she was suffering, so we had to put her down. I held her while they gave her the injection. It was very peaceful for her but really hard on me." Anna's lip began to tremble.

After sympathizing with Anna's loss, Isabel said, "You did absolutely the right thing. Letting animals die slowly because you can't bear to put them down is selfish, I think."

Isabel gave Ed a helpless glance hoping he might change the subject, but he appeared as much at a loss for words as she. Finally, she said, "Dr. Stewart, Ed was telling us that you are part of a chamber music quartet and that you get together once a week. That must be very enjoyable."

"Please call me Duncan. Yes, it is most enjoyable, although, I'm afraid that as of three days ago, we are down to a trio. Do you recall that power outage we had recently? Well, our pianist was rummaging around trying to find some candles and matches and became disoriented. He tripped over an ottoman and has fractured his wrist."

"Oh, that's a shame!" Anna said. "What will you do about the benefit? It's in a couple of weeks, isn't it?"

"Ten days to be exact. We were all set to play Mozart's Quartet in G Minor, but we'll have to cancel."

There was a silence. After a few seconds, Isabel realized that Anna and George were looking at her expectantly, and it didn't take her long to understand what they were thinking.

"Oh, no," she whispered softly shaking her head. "No."

"But, darling, you could…" George began.

"And it's for such a good cause," Anna said encouragingly. Turning to Duncan Stewart, she said, "Isabel doesn't just play the piano; she is a very accomplished musician. She could fill in."

Isabel felt acutely embarrassed. When she glanced up, Dr. Stewart was looking at her sympathetically. "You must feel that we are ganging up on you, but I swear to you this was not cooked up in advance. I hadn't told anyone here about the broken wrist. You certainly mustn't feel under any obligation. But if you would like to help out, we would welcome you."

"But you've never even heard me play," Isabel began.

"Maybe it would be best to let you think it over and let

me know in a couple of days? I feel we have no right to pressure you this way."

"Fine. I'll do that... and thank you," she added gratefully.

After a dessert of homemade coconut cream pie which Anna served because she knew George was fond of coconut in nearly any form, Isabel helped Anna clear the table, and soon everyone gathered in the living room to listen to Duncan and Isabel perform. Duncan played an air by Bach and a piece by Schumann. Isabel played a Chopin étude and Bach's Prelude in C Major. They then agreed to shift to something lighter and began "Danny Boy" together. After some coaxing, Anna, who was a member of the choir, sang along. Isabel noticed that, as he had promised, George was sitting near the door. She gave him the prearranged signal, and he slipped out when the piece was nearly over. As Duncan, Isabel and Anna finished, Ed applauded heartily. Isabel heard a dog's bark just outside and smiled. When George brought Sunshine into the living room, he handed Ed the leash, and the dog promptly lay down at Ed's feet.

Anna was starting to say something to Isabel when she saw Sunshine and stopped, speechless.

Ed said, "Darling, this is Sunshine. She's from the shelter and she needs a home. We thought you might like to give her one."

Anna said, "Oh, she's so beautiful!" and then, never taking her eyes from Sunshine's face, she approached her slowly, saying gently "Hello, Sunshine. Hello, my lovely girl," until she was able to kneel beside her and stroke her head. Sunshine wagged her tail appreciatively.

"You were in on this, too, weren't you, Isabel?" Anna said, her eyes brimming with happiness. "I didn't suspect a thing. How can I ever thank you?"

Later, as they were preparing for bed, Isabel commented, "I would say this evening was a resounding success."

"Yes, it was," George replied as he switched off the light.

Isabel said, "I think I'll do it, George."

"What?"

"Help out with the benefit."

"Good. I thought you would," George answered. He was soon asleep but Isabel lay awake for another half hour staring into the darkness.

Duncan Stewart was delighted to receive Isabel's call the next day. "It really is awfully good of you to do this," he said.

"I assume you play with the music in front of you?" Isabel asked. "I doubt that I could memorize the whole quartet in the time that's left."

"You won't need to memorize anything. We do play with the music. Now, I guess the next order of business is to get the music to you and to set up a few rehearsal times."

"I have my calendar here if you would like to suggest some dates."

Duncan said he would get back to Isabel after he spoke to the other two doctors. "They will be enormously pleased. I haven't told them we might be able to play the benefit, so this will come as a complete surprise."

The quartet met in a large old faculty house near the campus. Duncan Stewart insisted that Isabel pull up in front of this house and that he go with her to find a parking space and walk back to the house with her. "This can be a dangerous neighborhood, particularly in the evening," he said. "I don't want you walking alone."

Isabel liked the other two doctors immediately. One was an elderly neurologist who played the viola and the second was an ear, nose and throat specialist in his mid-thirties who was the cellist. They were all very complimentary when Isabel first played with them.

Isabel sighed and shook her head and said, "Well, that wasn't bad for a first run through, I guess. It should be better by the time of the concert."

Duncan Stewart unfailingly walked Isabel to her car after each rehearsal. When saying goodbye, he solemnly shook her hand in what she could only think of as a rather courtly manner, and he always went out of his way to thank her. Isabel was very glad that she had agreed to help these three doctors. It did not take her long to realize how unkind it would have been to refuse.

After the second rehearsal, as they were approaching Isabel's car, Duncan Stewart said, "I was browsing through the used-books section of a bookstore yesterday and found a dog-eared copy of T. S. Eliot's *Four Quartets*. I stayed up until midnight trying to make sense of it."

"It isn't easy," Isabel replied. "The poems are wonderful, but no one would call them easy."

"I felt out of my depth, and was nearly ready to give up. But I remembered that you enjoy poetry. I was hoping you might help enlighten me."

"Of course, if I can…"

"The preface said they are the last important poems Eliot wrote – a sort of summing up?"

"Yes, he…"

"They are…"

Laughing as they both began speaking at once, Isabel insisted that Duncan continue.

WHILE THE MUSIC LASTS

"They are meant to be religious?" he asked. "I know Eliot became an Anglican."

"My English professor said they can be seen as religious and philosophical but not devotional. It took me awhile to understand the difference. What he meant was that the poems are not to be seen as too narrowly or overtly Christian. Eliot believed that most people, living in time, have intuitions of the timeless."

"Not just Christians?"

"Right, not just Christians. And he also saw the relation of poetry to music: the analogy of the development of a theme…"

"In both?"

Isabel nodded. "He believed the transitions in a poem were comparable to the movements of a symphony or a quartet."

Duncan Stewart thought about this for a moment. "When you say that, it casts the poems in an entirely new light."

"And Eliot did counterpoint, too: desire versus love… nature versus grace."

"He did a lot with opposites, didn't he? 'In my beginning is my end' and so on."

"Exactly," Isabel smiled. "Until, finally, all opposites are brought together and everything becomes, as Eliot puts it, 'one'." Isabel offered her hand. "I haven't talked like this since my seminar with Professor Traversi," she said softly, "but I love reading Eliot."

"Thank you for these insights on the book. Frankly, I was getting nowhere on my own."

Isabel unlocked her car. "I think it's great that you wanted to read it." As she said this, she was somehow certain that he had chosen the book, at least in part, to have a conversational topic in common with her. How could she show him that she was pleased and that she appreciated his effort? "I can't imagine how I would react if someone put a complex medical textbook in front of me!" she exclaimed.

Dr. Stewart laughed. As he was helping her into the car, he warned suddenly, "Your dress will be caught in the door!"

Tucking her skirt around her knees, Isabel thanked him and started the engine. She waved good-bye as she pulled away and, glancing in her rear-view mirror, she saw Duncan Stewart wave back and remain standing beneath the streetlight until he was sure she was safely on her way.

The evening of the concert, Isabel unexpectedly developed a case of stage fright. Playing in church in front of the parishioners never bothered her. But it had been years since she had performed before a large audience of strangers. Another thought fueling her worry was that she did not want to disappoint these doctors who had been so very nice to her. As she stood waiting to go on, her hands were clammy, she was biting her lower lip and trembling slightly.

Duncan Stewart was somehow aware of her anxiety because he came and stood next to her and put his hand on her shoulder. "It will be fine," he said. "Please don't worry; I know it will go well. Just take a few deep breaths."

Isabel managed a slight smile and did as he told her. She was amazed that he had gauged her mood so accurately. "Thank you," she said. "I just don't want to let all of you down."

"You won't. I can guarantee that," he replied and gave her a warm smile of reassurance. He seemed so confident that Isabel allowed herself to believe that he might be right.

As they walked onstage, Isabel felt the fear begin to leave. Just before they began to play, she smiled at Duncan Stewart as if to say, "I'm okay now." He returned her smile as if to reply, "I know you are."

The performance was far better than any of the rehearsals had been. Isabel knew that actually having an audience provided an additional needed incentive. When they finished, the audience broke into spontaneous, lasting applause. In the wings, Isabel hugged each doctor, and there were comments of "We did it!" and "You were great!"

As she was getting ready to join George in the lobby, the fourth regular member of the quartet, his arm in a cast and a sling came backstage to congratulate everyone and particularly to praise and thank Isabel. "I think I should resign and let you take my place permanently!" he said.

Isabel laughed. "This once was fine, but I won't make a habit of it, if it's all the same to you!"

———

George was preparing for the midnight Christmas Eve service when a card arrived in the mail from the rector of Pembroke College, Oxford. The rector ended his message by saying, "When are you and Isabel going to visit us? If you could see your way clear to come at the end of spring term, Beth and I would be delighted to entertain you."

When George showed Isabel the card, which had a photograph of the altar in Pembroke's chapel, she said, "Could we go, George? I would love to see Oxford from the inside. I know how much it meant to you, and I've read so many novels and seen so many films where the characters are either at Oxford or Cambridge, that it would be wonderful to see it for myself."

"And I suppose an extra week of sightseeing in London wouldn't be amiss?" George smiled.

Isabel could hardly contain her enthusiasm but stopped suddenly and said, "Oh, but Emily will still be in school then."

George said, "Yes, of course, that's right, and I doubt asking the rector to postpone until her summer vacation would work. At her age, Emily wouldn't want to be dragged around London and an English university. She would much rather be with her friends." He paused, "Wait a minute! I'll call Alice tomorrow and see if she might be free to come and stay."

"Great idea!" Isabel exclaimed. "Emily loves being with her and vice versa."

The next day, Alice accepted with alacrity. "It will be wonderful to spend two weeks with Emily next spring!" she said. "But I warn you, I may spoil her rotten while you're away!"

"We'll take that chance," Isabel replied happily.

Alice, who had been so eager to see Isabel and George marry, was unmarried herself for over a decade after their wedding. Isabel often teased her gently, saying, "For someone who was such an excellent matchmaker, you are certainly taking your time!"

Alice would laugh and reply, "A good man is hard to find, and I just haven't met the right one yet."

Then, two years before, Isabel had answered the phone to hear an ebullient Alice on the line.

"Isabel," she said, "I'm eloping tomorrow! You know Charles Standish, the Washington D.C. lawyer I introduced to you when you came to visit me a couple of months ago?

We're getting married!"

"You're eloping?"

"Yes," Alice continued. "Charles is a widower, you know, and he's twelve years older than I am. Neither of us wants any sort of fuss. We're just going to the registry office tomorrow morning; then, we're catching an evening flight to Switzerland for our honeymoon."

Isabel was both surprised and delighted and was starting to say "how wonderful" when George walked into the room.

"I heard you say someone's eloping. Who is it?" he asked.

"It's Alice! It's your sister!"

George took the phone and said, "Well, It's about time, Sis! Who's the lucky man?"

Isabel went to get on another line and there was much hearty banter, laughter and congratulations.

Alice and her new husband lived happily for nearly two years until he suffered a major stroke. After lingering for three weeks, he died. He had left Alice extremely well off financially, but he had been unable to give her the child they both wanted. She was still in the process of trying to heal the pain from her devastating loss. Coming to stay with Emily would give her something to look forward to.

The confines of her Venetian hotel room, spacious though it was, were beginning to weigh on Isabel. From the terrace beneath, she heard the sounds of waiters placing china and silverware on tables, readying them for lunch. Although it was late summer, the warmth of the sun still invited people to dine al fresco. But the thought of food was the last thing on Isabel's mind. This was the afternoon when she would irrevocably set her plan in motion. She sat in front of the mirror and decided to dress so that it was unlikely she could be identified. Only one man might recognize her, but on this day, she was unwilling to chance encountering him. She brushed her still short hair up and away from her forehead and neck. Reaching for a large-brimmed straw hat, she wore it at an angle that partially hid her eyes. She rose from her chair, took her full-length lightweight coat from a hanger and slipped it on. She had lost so much weight that the coat was now at least two sizes too large, but as she caught a glimpse of her reflection, she thought the extra fabric nicely obscured her rather gaunt figure. As soon as she was outdoors, a pair of dark glasses would complete her outfit. She ignored the small voice in her head that told her these efforts to disguise herself were patently absurd.

Looking directly across the Grand Canal, she saw the imposing Basilica of Santa Maria della Salute. Isabel had read in her tourist guide that its first stone had been laid in 1631 in homage and gratitude to the Virgin Mary for the end of a plague that had devastated the city. From this beginning, the exuberantly ornate, octagonal structure, which echoed both the Byzantine Middle Ages and the architecture of Palladio, rose to prominence on the edge of St. Mark's basin. Its white stone gleaming in the sunlight, the basilica seemed almost to beckon to Isabel, and impulsively, she decided to take a gondola across the canal and ask the gondolier to wait while she made a brief visit to the sanctuary.

The basilica's interior, when compared to its lavish exterior, was cold and austere. Isabel shivered and wondered why she had been drawn to this place. Was she trying to bargain with God? Was she asking for His blessing when she knew that to do so would be blasphemous? She watched an old man light a candle at one of the altars and decided that she needed to do the same. After she put some money in the collection box, she picked up a burning candle and tried to use it to light a fresh one. But she was clumsy in her attempt, and a bit of hot wax fell on her hand while more dripped on the floor. Isabel took this as a sign of condemnation and tears welled in her eyes. She turned to leave, but just at that moment, the organist began to practice and he was playing Bach. As the sound reverberated joyfully through the immense space, Isabel regained her composure. When the fugue was finished, she walked back to her gondola with new determination. She told the gondolier to take her across the canal to St. Mark's Square. There she tipped him handsomely, and keeping her wallet in her hand, she walked to the vaporetto stop to buy a ticket that would take her as far as the Lido.

As the large jet began its race down the runway, Isabel looked out of the window to see New York receding beneath them as they became airborne. She reached over to squeeze George's hand. "This is marvelous," she said. "I'm so grateful to you for making it possible."

George smiled at her indulgently. "I hope they give us dinner soon. I'm getting hungry," he said.

They quickly found that they would have to make do with two bags of peanuts during the long and very leisurely "drinks hour." It was quite late by New York time when dinner finally arrived.

"I realize they like to stretch things out because they

want to keep us from getting bored, but I have absolutely no intention of watching the movie, now. I'd like to get some sleep before we arrive in London," George said.

"I think I'm too excited to sleep," Isabel answered. She decided to try the film but found it rather inane and predictable fare with a lot of physical comedy. Switching her headphone channel to classical music, she closed her eyes. "It's only a few hours away now," she thought. "England!"

George, as a priest of the American Episcopal church, was also a member of the worldwide Anglican communion under the supervision of the Archbishop of Canterbury. As such, when they arrived in London, he was able to give Isabel a tour of Lambeth Palace, the official home of the Archbishop. The red-brick exterior dated from the late fifteenth century. Although there had been much renovation of the interior in the nineteenth century, Isabel was able to gain a real sense of the original edifice from the main hall which, built around 1660, housed a superb collection of illuminated manuscripts and rare books.

Later the same day, George took her to St. Paul's Cathedral where they met an elderly and loquacious gentleman who told them, among other things, that he had been on the bucket fire brigade on the Cathedral's dome during the blitz of World War II.

At Westminster Abbey, Isabel lingered in the Poets' Corner and it was there she decided that, since George had some church business to attend to, she would map out a literary tour for herself of famous writers' homes and haunts and see as many of them as time would permit. She went through Dickens' and Carlyle's houses. She strolled for blocks down Cheyne Walk admiring the spectacularly beautiful Georgian architecture of the town houses with their front gardens and palatial, high wrought-iron gates overlooking the Thames.

She walked around Bloomsbury and spent a day in the British Museum. Each evening, she returned to her hotel exhausted but full of new experiences to share with George.

At the end of a week, they went to Paddington Station to board the train for Oxford. The rector had told them to come directly to Pembroke where he planned to have them stay in a suite of rooms.

The taxi pulled up before the large double doors of the college. Student bicycles either stood bunched together outside or were leaning against the walls. George pushed the bell button and a smaller door, cut into the larger doors, opened, and they were admitted. The porter rang for the rector while George and Isabel waited in the courtyard. The day, which had threatened rain earlier, had become partly cloudy with sunny intervals.

"So this is where you lived," Isabel reflected. "It's absolutely lovely!"

In a few moments, the rector and his wife appeared and greeted them warmly. The rector was of average height and portly; his wife was plump and had a flawless complexion.

"Please follow us," they said as they walked down the courtyard and passed through a door that led to the Master's Garden. They turned left and went up a flight of stairs and saw two doors one of which was labeled "Master's Study"; the other had "The Salt Room" written above it. The rector opened this door and they walked into a living room. There was a sofa, and two overstuffed chairs were near the fireplace. A small dining table had straight chairs at each end, and in the corner was a built-in bookcase which housed various volumes, several on the history of Oxford. A telephone table stood beneath the windows through which they could look down on the Master's Garden. Old prints of the University hung on the off-white walls.

The rector's wife turned to the left into a bedroom that had a double bed in one corner. There was a sink with a mirror above it just to the right as you entered. A bureau was straight ahead and a wardrobe was to the left. The living room and bedroom were warmed by a deep red wall-to-wall carpet.

"This is delightful – so spacious!" Isabel murmured.

The rector opened a door to the right of the wardrobe. "The bath is in here," he said. This smaller room held a very large, high old bathtub with a recent, rather makeshift, shower attachment. Isabel noted that there seemed to be no toilet. Soon, she and George were walking back through the living room and down a small corridor to the right. This led to an old-fashioned but serviceable kitchen which had a small refrigerator stocked with bread, milk and juice. Bowls, cups and plates were in the cupboards as well as boxes of hot and cold cereals.

"The saucepans are in this cupboard and the silverware is in this drawer. I think you will find everything you need here for breakfast," the rector's wife smiled at them.

On the way down the corridor to the kitchen, Isabel saw a door that was slightly ajar, and within, she could just see a very old toilet with its tank near the ceiling from which was hanging a long pull chain.

Noticing her glance, the rector's wife apologized. "I'm sorry the plumbing is so antiquated."

Isabel was quick to say, "Oh, no, not at all." She decided to leave it at that but she was thinking that the old plumbing was exactly right. Anything more modern would tend to mar the remarkable ambience.

Before she could speak again, they heard the loud, melodious chime of a clock.

"That's Old Tom," the rector said, "in the tower of Christ Church College which is directly across from us here."

"What a beautiful sound!" Isabel said. She was enchanted and could scarcely believe where she was.

"If you will join us in the common room at six, we will have sherry before dinner. Tonight we will be going to High Table which is being given to honor some of the history graduates."

George and Isabel thanked their hosts. They rested for an hour, tired from their busy week in London and the train journey to Oxford. After they dressed for dinner, George said, "We have twenty minutes before we meet everyone for sherry. There is something I would like to show you first."

He led Isabel downstairs and out across the courtyard to the chapel. As they entered, Isabel was awed by the Gothic splendor and spoke in a hushed voice, even though she and George were the only people there.

"This is the place where you decided to become an Episcopal priest, isn't it?" she asked.

"Yes," George replied. "I so wanted you to see it. I just wish Emily were here too."

"You must show her one day when she is older, when she can truly appreciate it."

"We will show her together," George said, taking Isabel's hand and leading her into a pew.

They sat together in silence until it was time to join the others.

WHILE THE MUSIC LASTS

The common room, which was large with tall, ornate windows, held comfortable sofas and chairs. Sherry and glasses were on a side table along the wall. Faculty, dressed in academic robes, mingled with graduating students and guests. The rector and his wife made all of the necessary introductions.

After a short while, the rector led George and Isabel up some stairs to a balcony where, lying on the floor, were several magnificent leaded-glass windows in various states of disrepair.

"We are not sure what to do with these," the rector said. "It is prohibitively expensive to restore them."

Isabel exclaimed at their beauty.

George said, "I'm certain some American church would love to have them. If you would like, I can make inquiries when we return."

"Thank you, that would be helpful," the rector replied.

"The church in Westport!" Isabel said. "The committee has just hired an architect to draw up plans for the new wing. Maybe he could incorporate these windows somehow."

"My wife has a real gift for taking old things and giving them new life," George said proudly. "You should see the work she did on our parsonage."

"Perhaps we can take some measurements and snap some photos to take back with us?" Isabel asked.

"Of course," the rector replied.

The large, high-ceilinged dining hall with various colorful academic banners flying from the rafters was everything Isabel had imagined it would be. The undergraduates were all seated at long tables. The rector, his wife, George, Isabel and the other guests made their way through the undergraduates, on their way to the high table which was on a dais at the far end of the hall. Everyone

WHILE THE MUSIC LASTS

remained standing for the prayer, given in Latin.

During the first course of prawn cocktail, Isabel talked with a student to her right who was an American. He had matriculated at Oxford because he wished to specialize in sixteenth-century English history and was planning to stay to take an advanced degree.

Soon the conversation broadened to include all of those near Isabel and George, and the topic of American politics came up. Several guests wanted to know what they thought of recent headlines from the White House.

Isabel smiled and said, "You have to realize that I was brought up in a very liberal, Democratic family and, to this day, my views are colored by that perspective. If you wish to hear someone more moderate - not conservative, mind you, but moderate - I think I should defer to my husband."

George laughed. "She defers to me in conversation, but never if I make even the slightest attempt to influence her vote. Which is, of course, exactly as it should be."

After the entrée of filet mignon, potatoes and mixed vegetables, the rector stood and said, "Please keep your napkins, and we will adjourn for dessert."

They went, napkins in hand, back out to the courtyard and down to another door that led to a dining room that had a large, mahogany dining table and chairs for twelve. Isabel noticed that the walls were covered in a deep, hunter green brocade paper and that large oil portraits of personages of distinction hung in heavy, gilt frames around the room.

They were invited to sit at the table where blanc-mange was soon brought by the staff wearing white jackets. Following the pudding, fruit and cheese were passed.

Isabel talked with a member of the history faculty. She told him how much she and George had enjoyed the Inspector Morse mysteries set in Oxford and that they were sorry when the series ended and when they read that John Thaw, who played Morse, had died not long after the final episode.

The history don said, "Those of us who live in Oxford often found that series amusing because Morse would set off from one location in his red Jaguar and end up in another which he could not possibly have reached by going the direction he did."

Isabel smiled. "Of course, we Americans never noticed."

Small chocolates, wrapped in deep blue paper with "Pembroke College" written on them, were passed on silver trays. Brandy was sent around the table twice as was snuff. Isabel accepted a brandy but declined the offer of snuff.

Finally, there were finger bowls and Isabel was grateful to her grandmother who, when she was an adolescent, had shown her how to dip the tips of her fingers on one hand into the bowl and wipe them on her napkin and repeat the same process with the other hand. At the time, Isabel had thought the lesson was a foolish anachronism that she would never use.

It was a warm, clear night, and everyone lingered in the courtyard after dessert, finishing conversations, making plans and saying good night. When George and Isabel climbed the steps to the Salt Room, she commented that it had been a perfect evening and one that she would never forget. She hugged George and thanked him.

They decided that George would take the side of the bed next to the wall because he was such a sound sleeper. Isabel, if she had insomnia, sometimes got up in the night to read and didn't want to have to crawl over George in the process. This evening, however, she soon drifted off while happily reviewing the highlights of their trip. In the morning, they planned to visit the Ashmolean before returning to London.

At four a.m., Isabel woke with a sharp pain in her stomach. She slipped out of bed and went into the living room, quietly closing the door behind her. If she could walk up and down, she thought, the pain might pass. She paced the floor; the light coming through the window from a lamp near the Master's Garden was sufficient to see, and she stopped now and then to look out, wanting to remember everything about this experience of being at Pembroke.

The pain was stubborn and Isabel began to feel very nauseated. She ran to the W.C. and tried to vomit without much success. Feeling utterly exhausted, she curled up on the sofa so as not to disturb George if she had to get up again and, finally, fell asleep. George found her there in the morning.

"Isabel," he said, "what are you doing out here?"

"Oh, it's nothing," Isabel replied. "I wasn't able to sleep and didn't want to wake you."

"You're looking very pale. Are you sure you are all right?"

"Yes, after my shower and a little breakfast, I should be fine." She did not mention that she was still in some pain.

"I'll fix breakfast while you dress, then," George said. "Even I know how to boil oatmeal."

Isabel toyed with her cereal and sent George off to the Ashmolean alone, telling him she would rather stay and have a quiet morning. She packed their overnight bag and asked the maid to do up the room later. She found one of the more concise histories of Oxford in the bookcase, took it back to the bedroom along with a cup of tea and climbed back into bed, propping herself up on pillows.

George returned about noon. They had a light lunch

WHILE THE MUSIC LASTS

and bade farewell to the rector and his wife, extracting a promise that they would visit them in America before too long.

George read a newspaper and Isabel looked out the window on the train back to London. She was still feeling queasy but was determined not to worry George. They were flying home in a few days, and she was looking forward to seeing Emily and Alice.

That night in the hotel, Isabel again was awake with pain and nausea. She was up and in the bathroom early when George woke and found her gone from the room. He knocked on the bathroom door and opened it to discover her sitting on the floor by the toilet.

"I'm sorry," Isabel said. "I'm sorry, George. I don't know what's wrong. Maybe we should try for an earlier flight home."

But George was having none of it. "I'm getting you to a doctor," he said. He called the American embassy, described Isabel's condition, and asked for a referral to a physician. He was given the name of a specialist in internal medicine on Harley Street who agreed to see Isabel that afternoon.

Isabel was surprised to learn that going to see a doctor on Harley Street was essentially to enter a very elegant London townhouse. George rapped the gleaming brass lion's head knocker that shone all the more against the glossy black paint of the large exterior door. A woman in a black uniform with a white apron asked if she could help them.

George said, "Mrs. Larsson to see Dr. Campbell."

"Yes, please follow me," the woman said, leading them across the diamond patterned, black and white marble floor and opening another door into what gave every appearance of being a drawing room but which was, in fact, the waiting room. The floor was covered with a large Aubusson rug. The upholstery on the sofas and chairs took the colors of soft blue and mauve from this carpet. Blue silk moiré draperies hung at the tall windows facing the street. There was a sofa table with current periodicals arranged neatly in rows. Above the ornate mantel, which was carved in an Adam design with a vase motif in the center, hung a large oil painting of a rural landscape in an elaborate, gilded frame.

Isabel realized at once that she was experiencing one aspect of Britain's private health care system. She knew the public health establishment had a reputation for being Spartan.

After a short while, the woman in the uniform reappeared and said, "Mrs. Larsson, will you come with me, please?"

Isabel went halfway down the entrance hall to a small elevator. Its cage was embellished with minutely worked scrolls of decorative wrought iron. There was a little seat inside, upholstered in powder blue velvet, with a Regency mirror hanging above it. The woman told Isabel to push the button marked two.

On floor two, the elevator opened into a small waiting area. Almost immediately, Dr. Campbell came out of his consulting room and offered Isabel a chair opposite him as he moved to sit behind his desk. He asked her, in a distinctly American accent, to describe her symptoms - an accent she could not help remarking upon because it seemed out of place in the quintessentially English surroundings.

Dr. Campbell smiled. "Yes," he said, "I'm from New Hampshire originally. My wife is English."

Isabel told him about the nausea and the pain which continually seemed to bore into her back.

Dr. Campbell asked several questions and wrote some detailed notes. He pushed a button and a nurse appeared.

"Mrs. Larsson," he said, "I'd like to examine you. Nurse Jennings will assist you."

Isabel went into an anteroom, disrobed and was prepared by the nurse to lie on the table. Dr. Campbell's examination was thorough but not overly long. Soon she was dressed again and back in the consulting room.

"Mrs. Larsson," the doctor said, "I'd like to put you in a nursing home for a few days and do some tests."

"A nursing home?" Isabel repeated skeptically.

"Yes," Dr. Campbell said. "But it's nothing like an American one, I assure you. Depending on the results of the tests, it might be advisable to do exploratory surgery."

Arrangements were made for Isabel to enter a home on Welbeck Street that runs parallel to Harley Street, two blocks to the West. George took her there in a taxi and had the cab wait while he helped her inside. He and Isabel agreed that he should return to the hotel to pack a small bag of her things. She looked pale and a little frightened as she wrote a list and handed it to him. Glancing at the paper, George said, "Don't worry, I'll be back with these in no time!" He kissed her on the cheek and said, "See you shortly!"

Isabel was given a quiet room on the top floor at the back where she could look out over the rooftops. The room was large and cheerful. The walls were painted a pale turquoise. There was a single bed and a nightstand with a lamp and telephone. Two comfortable club chairs were by the fireplace, and there was a desk with a chair in the bay window that had long, colorful floral chintz draperies at each end that could be pulled across the window at night. The room belied its function as a place for someone who was ill, resembling instead a charming room in a private home. The only clue that it was a medical facility was a row of call buttons for the nursing staff next to the headboard.

Isabel had asked George to bring the book she was reading and some magazines. When she was not reading, she looked out the window at the primarily rainy weather. She noticed that each evening, around five o'clock, there were a few feeble rays of sun that broke through the clouds before night descended. She wondered what could be wrong with her and thought about her mother's early death. She knew these ideas were morbid, and she tried not to dwell on them. She thought about Elizabeth Barrett Browning who had been ill in her home on Wimpole Street, not far from where Isabel now lay.

The various medical tests proved inconclusive, although Dr. Campbell said there seemed to be some anomaly on Isabel's pancreas. He wanted to go ahead with exploratory surgery.

"No, I'm sorry," Isabel said. "I want you to patch me up and give me some pain medication – whatever it takes to get me home. If I have to have surgery, I want to be home."

Dr. Campbell did his best to persuade her to stay but Isabel was adamant. Finally he said, "Yes, I can give you pain medication, but it will make you drowsy. I want you to use wheelchairs at the airports. And under no circumstances can you travel alone."

"I will be with her," George said.

"In that case, fine," Mr. Campbell replied. "I'll have the results of the tests we've performed ready for you to take with you. You can give them to your American doctor."

WHILE THE MUSIC LASTS

George had telephoned Alice, and she was waiting for them at the airport. Emily was spending the afternoon with a neighbor. Alice had prepared her to the extent that she had told her, "Mummy is sick. She will be very tired when she gets home and will need a lot of rest. So we will have to remember to be quiet. All right?"

Emily had nodded solemnly. "What's wrong with her?"

"We're not sure. She had a few tests in England, but when they wanted to do more, she told them no, that she just wanted to go home and see her own doctor. That made sense, didn't it?" Alice said, giving Emily a reassuring smile.

Isabel went to bed as soon as she arrived. She woke several hours later to find George sleeping beside her. She lay quietly thinking about what was ahead of her. Alice was her mainstay. Isabel knew she could trust her completely to help if she had to have surgery.

Alice had made an appointment for Isabel with Ed Marsden. He read over the reports from England and ordered some tests of his own.

When Isabel sat down in his office, he was very serious. "I think the British people had the right idea. The only way we can determine for certain what is going on with your pancreas is to do a laparoscopy, which is minimally invasive abdominal surgery. Then, depending on what we find, we may do a biopsy. I'm sorry, Isabel. I know that's not what you were hoping to hear."

Isabel sighed. "Well, at least I'm home. Can we do it soon? I'd just like to get it over with."

"Yes, I'll set you up with my colleague, Dr. Snyder.

He's a good man – a fine surgeon."

Isabel was given an injection in her hospital room to calm her, and she remembered being wheeled into the operating room but nothing of what happened after she arrived there. She felt she was somewhere very dark, very pleasant, very safe, and wherever the place was, she did not wish to leave it. But there was an annoying woman's voice close to her ear saying, "Wake up, Mrs. Larsson. The surgery is over. It's time to wake up now."

Isabel opened her eyes and saw a nurse standing by her bed. She was back in her hospital room. "How did it go?" she asked the nurse. "What did they find?"

"Dr. Snyder will be in later to talk with you and your husband."

"Can't you tell me anything?"

"No, you will have to wait and talk with the doctor. He has prescribed medication for post-operative pain. I can give you that now if you like."

"Fine," Isabel said and closed her eyes. The pain medication made her drowsy and she soon went back to sleep. When she awoke, George was sitting next to her bed.

"Hello, dear," she said. "Have you been here long?"

"No, not very long. Visiting hours started a few minutes ago. How are you feeling?"

"Pretty well considering I had an operation this morning. They've given me something for pain. Have you seen the doctor? I don't know how everything went. The nurse couldn't tell me anything."

"Dr. Snyder's office called the parsonage. His receptionist wanted to be sure I would be here during visiting hours, so he could talk to both of us." George had barely finished saying this when Dr. Snyder walked into the room. He stood at the foot of Isabel's bed.

"Reverend and Mrs. Larsson," he began, "I'm afraid the news is not good." Looking directly at Isabel, he said, "We found a malignancy on your pancreas which has spread to some adjacent organs. We removed as much of it as we were able to. I recommend an intensive regimen of chemotherapy with the hope that we can put you into remission."

"Remission?" Isabel repeated.

"What does that mean exactly?" George asked.

"It means that you are symptom free," the doctor said.

Isabel pushed the button to raise the head of the bed so that she was sitting up more. From her experience of visiting parishioners with cancer, she thought she knew exactly what remission was. If remission lasted five years, a cancer could be said to be cured. But many of the parishioners had remissions that lasted only briefly and they died. She was not going to be fobbed off with the words "symptom free."

"Dr. Snyder," she said, speaking slowly and deliberately, "I'm going to ask you a question, and I want you to be completely candid. How many patients have you seen with pancreatic cancer – because that is what we are talking about – how many have you seen with a pancreas in the same state as mine who were still in remission five years after having treatment?"

Dr. Snyder seemed startled by the question. He cleared his throat and said, "You are talking about a cure. I'm afraid we can't use the word 'cure' here, but I recommend starting chemotherapy as soon as possible."

"My God, " Isabel thought, "he's telling me I'm dying but he won't just come out and say it." She felt as if she were having a nightmare and things around her appeared somehow glassy and unreal. "I see," she said.

After the initial shock, Isabel's thoughts raced. First she had to comfort George who looked stricken. Next, she had to be the one to explain all of this to Emily. She obtained a promise that no one would say anything to Emily until she had talked with her.

Isabel went home the next morning. She spent her last night in the hospital thinking about treatment and wondering if, indeed, she should go for treatment at all. Isabel did not want to be rushed into chemotherapy. A large part of her was inclined to forego this intensive and very difficult option just to gain a few more months of life. But, then, there were George and Emily to consider. Alice would be able to help her sort through all of this and make the correct choices.

George told Alice the truth after obtaining her promise that she would say nothing to Emily. Alice came to the hospital with George to pick up Isabel, and when she saw her sitting on the edge of the bed, dressed and ready to leave, she put her arms around her and hugged her. Neither of them spoke. They took the few things of Isabel's that were left in her room and carried them home in a plastic bag. After lunch, Alice fixed a tray with two mugs, a pot of tea and some cream and sugar, and took it into the living room.

"Emily believes in God and in heaven," Isabel was saying as she put her feet up on the sofa. "We will tell her that she will have to be very brave because God needs me. No, that sounds like something you would say to a small child. I can't talk down to her. I really can't find the words…" Isabel's voice trailed off. After a few seconds she said, "The thing I hate most about this whole thing is leaving Emily." Tears came to Isabel's eyes and she brushed them away impatiently. "I remember the shock when my own mother died suddenly. It was horrible. But then, thank God, she has you." She reached over and patted Alice' hand. Alice took her hand and squeezed it.

"We should talk about your treatment," Alice said. "The doctor said it should begin right away, didn't he?"

"Yes," Isabel acknowledged, "but treatment doesn't mean a cure, you know. The only hope is for remission - maybe a few good months if I'm lucky. I'm wondering if it's really worth putting myself through the aggressive chemotherapy it would take."

"That has to be your decision", Alice said.

"I think maybe I should do it for George and Emily's sake. It would give them more time to adjust."

"Yes, it would," Alice agreed. "Why don't you talk it over with the doctor you met through the Marsdens. Wasn't he an oncologist? "

"Duncan Stewart?" Isabel brightened visibly. "Of course... yes, absolutely! He's so very nice. If anyone can take me through chemotherapy, he can. I'll call and make an appointment to see him."

"I'll look up his number for you," Alice volunteered. She returned a few minutes later with the phone book and a cell phone. She dialed the number and handed the phone to Isabel.

"Yes, good afternoon. My name is Isabel Larsson and I'd like to make an appointment to see Dr. Stewart. Yes, I'd be a new patient..." Isabel paused and listened to the receptionist. "But I'm a friend. Yes I understand that, but would you please ask him to call me? Thank you very much." Isabel gave the receptionist her number and hung up. "He's not accepting any new patients. Apparently there was so much favorable press after his book came out that he's swamped. Was it wrong of me to use the fact that I know him to try to get in?"

"Of course not!" Alice said vehemently.

The phone rang and Isabel jumped. "Hello," she said. "Oh, Duncan, thank you so much for calling me back so quickly. I think I'm going to need your help. I have pancreatic cancer, and they tell me I might achieve remission but they don't hold out hope for a cure."

Duncan Stewart expressed his grave concern. His kind tone nearly reduced Isabel to tears. They spoke for a few more minutes, and Dr. Stewart said he would have his receptionist call her back right away. The result was that Isabel got an appointment with Dr. Stewart the next Tuesday at four o'clock.

Emily slammed the back door as she arrived home from school. She threw her backpack down on the kitchen counter, went to the refrigerator for a glass of milk, grabbed a bag of chocolate chip cookies and appeared at the entrance to the living room.

Isabel was still tucked up on the sofa with a wool throw over her knees and Alice was sitting in a chair beside her.

"Hello, sweetheart, how was your day?" Isabel inquired.

"Okay."

"Do you have a lot of homework?"

"The usual."

Emily came in and sat cross-legged on the floor. She ate three cookies and reached into the bag for a fourth. Normally, Isabel would have reminded her not to eat so many that she would spoil her appetite for dinner. But, since her diagnosis, she had given up the role of disciplinarian. Now, she wanted all of her interactions with Emily to be pleasant. Alice, sensing this, took up the gauntlet.

"Emily, dear," she said, "be sure you leave room for supper. I'm fixing spaghetti, and I know that's one of your favorites."

Emily said nothing but closed the bag of cookies and set it on the floor. Staring down at her hands, she said, "Why won't anyone tell me what is going on?"

Isabel shot a glance at Alice who mimed that she would leave, but Isabel shook her head and gave her a pleading look that begged her to stay.

"We need to talk," Isabel began.

"There's something bad going on," Emily said. "I can tell. People stop talking when I come into the room. Dad looks as if someone had hit him with a ton of bricks. And all of you are trying to act as if everything's normal. But it isn't normal is it?"

"No, " Isabel said, "it isn't. I wanted to decide what I was going to do before I talked with you."

"What you are going to do?"

"Yes. When I had my operation, they found cancer in my pancreas. They took out as much as they could but they couldn't get all of it which means, if I do nothing, that it will just grow back."

"So doing nothing's not an option, right?" Emily asked.

"No, I guess it isn't."

"You guess?"

Seeing the fear in Emily's eyes, Isabel knew that treatment was inevitable.

"I can start chemotherapy. I have an appointment with the doctor next Tuesday. Chemotherapy could put me into remission which means I could feel well again – at least for awhile – but it's not a permanent cure."

"How long would you be in remission?"

"I don't know. That's something I'll have to ask the doctor. I'm not sure he will know exactly."

Emily bent over and put her face in her hands.

"Oh, honey," Isabel said. I'm so terribly sorry. I wish I could be more comforting. If you were little I'd…"

"Do what?" Emily said fiercely. "Take me into the picture? Pretend we're in the gondola? But I'm too old for that ridiculous stuff, Mother! I'm too old!"

Emily got up and ran out of the room. Isabel and Alice heard her bedroom door shut and then the sound of Emily's sobs.

"Shall I go to her?" Alice asked.

"Not right now," Isabel replied. "She needs to cry. Oh, Alice, oh!" Isabel's own eyes filled with tears. Alice came and knelt beside her so that she could hold her close.

Duncan Stewart put down the phone and sighed. Although he often had to deal with terminally ill patients, Isabel's prognosis came as a shock. She was young, vibrant and very beautiful, and he cursed the fact that medicine, and that he in particular, had to stand by – essentially helpless – and watch the progression of this vile disease called cancer. The "war on cancer" had been going on for years and, although doctors and researchers had won some skirmishes, the enemy was far from defeated. Now, this lovely woman, who had every reason to expect many more good years of life, was to be cut down in her prime. He had seen his last patient for the day and had planned to spend time doing some paperwork in his office. Instead, he locked the papers in his desk drawer and decided to leave early.

Walking back toward his condominium, he passed

WHILE THE MUSIC LASTS

a fast food restaurant and, after a moment's hesitation, went in and ordered a double cheeseburger, French fries and a large chocolate malt. Normally very careful about his diet, tonight he would throw caution to the winds. He relished this greasy feast, and when he had finished, he allowed himself a comforting burp without his usual polite suppression of the sound.

When he left the restaurant, the weather had deteriorated. Wind was blowing in strong gusts, and it had begun to thunder. He bent his head into the gale and turned up the collar of his raincoat. The doorman at his condominium greeted him with a cheery "Good evening, doctor!" to which he responded "Good evening, Joe." But, as he pushed the elevator button for his floor, he thought that it was, in fact, not a good evening at all. Opening the door to his apartment, he paused for a moment and thought how singularly ugly this small space he called home really was. Lit only by the murky light of the grey sky outside, his few possessions seemed depressingly ordinary. He had taken the furniture and books from his bedroom in the New Canaan house and had found a small dinette set in a used furniture store; he placed this in his condominium's dining area. He bought himself a comfortable recliner that he used for reading and for listening to classical music, his chief forms of relaxation. He attempted nothing else; there were no pictures on the walls. He realized that he knew absolutely nothing about interior design and seriously doubted his aptitude should he develop the inclination to learn. Under the circumstances, he felt it was best to leave that side of things well enough alone. He filled the built-in bookcases with medical books and journals and, when he had used up the shelf space, he began piling books and papers in stacks on the dinette table, leaving himself barely enough room to eat. His meals, for the most part, consisted of frozen, microwaveable portions for one that he ate while reading the latest medical literature.

Soon after moving into his studio, he had begun work on his book on pain control. This meant that he lived medicine during even more of his waking hours and, consequently, that he gave even less thought to his surroundings. He was inherently practical and, for the most part, was content with only the most basic of creature comforts. This is not to say that he was entirely immune to the pleasures of feminine domesticity: well-cooked meals and agreeably furnished rooms. His mother had provided both in abundance, but, with her death, he felt that chapter in his life had ended.

Usually, he would turn on his stereo soon after entering the apartment. But, tonight, the pleasures of Mozart or Bach held little interest for him. When he thought of music, he thought of Isabel and the exceptionally delightful time they had had rehearsing for and then playing the benefit concert. She seemed to be everywhere in his consciousness this evening. He sank into a chair without even removing his raincoat.

He knew enough about psychiatry to realize that Freud would have attributed his penchant for constant work to sublimation of his early disappointment in love. If this diagnosis were correct, Duncan Stewart was indifferent to it. His interest in Freud was essentially that Freud's atheism had stemmed, in part, from his equating the dilemma of pain in the world so much with evil, that it left him unable to believe in any loving or merciful God.

The mental jury in Dr. Stewart's mind was still out on the question of God. As Charlie Rose had pointed out, his area of expertise, oncology, often brought him very close to suffering. But he could not forget the good he had seen alongside the pain. Dying patients were often noble in their efforts to spare their loved ones unnecessary anguish. This nobility of spirit never failed to move him. If there were no God, where did such fortitude and self-subordination arise?

He was currently reading C.S. Lewis's *The Problem of Pain* and *A Grief Observed*, the latter of which Lewis wrote after the death of his wife from cancer. Lewis had worked through the issue of pain and had maintained his conversion from atheism to Christianity. So where did the truth about religion lie? Duncan Stewart was still uncertain.

Alice was in bed with the flu. She had planned to drive Isabel to the Grace-New Haven Hospital for her appointment, but as her fever climbed to one hundred and two degrees, it was obvious that she would be unable to go. George had an important meeting with the bishop that he offered to cancel, but Isabel would not hear of it.

"This is my first appointment," she said. "I checked and I won't be having chemotherapy today. There is absolutely no reason why I can't drive myself."

Isabel allotted twice the amount of time it would take to drive to the hospital, allowing for any contingencies of traffic or roadwork. Feeling that her appointment was on sufferance, she was already embarrassed and was not about to compound this by being late.

She walked into the hospital lobby and went directly to the doctors' information board. She found the floor and number of Dr. Stewart's office and decided to sit in the lobby until closer to the time for her appointment.

Earlier, busy studying the road map and readying herself to see Duncan Stewart, she had skipped lunch and now realized this had been a mistake. She felt very empty and her stomach was emitting frequent loud growls. She went to the reception desk to ask if there were a place to get a snack and was directed to the hospital cafeteria.

Passing by dishes of pasta, beef stroganoff and salads with heavy dressings, Isabel settled for a bowl of tomato vegetable soup and a cup of tea. She had brought along the new edition from the University of Pennsylvania Press of Theodore Dreiser's *Jennie Gerhardt*. This edition announced that it had restored 16,000 words cut by Harper and Brothers in 1911 because they were worried about the book's "moral stance." Despite this titillating disclosure, Isabel was proven correct in her assumption that the work would be tame by modern standards. She read the same paragraph over and over, and when, after fifteen minutes, she found herself still on the same page, she gave up and closed the book. She couldn't concentrate. She drank the last of her tea watching the hands of the cafeteria clock inch toward four o'clock.

As Isabel entered, the receptionist in Dr. Stewart's office smiled in a friendly manner. She was in her late fifties, Isabel guessed, plump and blue eyed, her once blonde hair now heavily streaked with grey.

"Good afternoon, Mrs. Larsson," she said pleasantly. "May I have your insurance card, please, and ask you to fill out these patient information papers?" She handed Isabel a clipboard.

"Yes, of course." Isabel sat and filled out the questionnaire on her medical history. She had barely finished when the office door opened and Duncan Stewart walked into the waiting room.

"Isabel," he said, taking her hand. "It is always a pleasure to see you, although I wish it weren't under these circumstances."

He stood aside, motioning Isabel to the chair opposite his desk in the office and closed the door behind her.

Isabel said, "Thank you so much for seeing me. I'm afraid I took advantage of our friendship to get to see you, and I want to apologize for that."

"Oh, not at all," Dr. Stewart said. "I very much dislike having to turn any patients away. This is something that has been thrust on me just recently because I published the book. Fortunately, Mabel, my receptionist, does most of the dirty work for me."

"Your book was excellent. I can understand why people want you to be their physician."

"When I first met you, I was surprised when you said you had read my book. Why did the problem of pain control interest you then?"

"I volunteered in the pediatric ward of our local hospital and saw what, as a lay person, I believed to be insufficient pain relief for some of the children. I was very concerned. So your book struck a chord."

"Ah, yes, I understand."

Dr. Stewart began asking about Isabel's experience in England and her treatment to date, taking careful notes as she answered his questions. This went on routinely for a few minutes. Finally Duncan Stewart looked up and said, "If it is agreeable with you, we can start your chemotherapy in three days. I hope you will be able to have someone drive you to and from the hospital. It is never certain just when side effects may begin, and I don't want you on the highway alone."

"My sister-in-law will be with me."

"Good." Duncan Stewart stood, came around the desk and took both of Isabel's hands in his. "The road to remission can be a very grueling journey, but I will do everything in my power to help you." He took a small pad from the desk and wrote a number on it. Tearing off the sheet, he said, "Here. This is my home phone number. Please feel free to call me whenever you feel the need for reassurance, and please don't worry about waking me."

"Thank you so much," Isabel replied. "I..." she hesitated.

"Yes?"

"I should tell you that I debated whether or not to have treatment because I know it won't be a cure. But when I saw my daughter's face... when I told her how sick I was, I knew she would want me to make every effort."

"In all candor, I believe that most of my patients ultimately are glad they put themselves through treatment. They are grateful for the extra time to get their affairs in order. Remission allows them a certain peace. Some people use the time to do things they have always wanted to do but just never did."

As she drove home, Isabel realized how fortunate she was to be under the care of such a doctor. She was frightened of her approaching therapy, but she thought that, with his help, she could complete it.

The rigor of taking the cancer-killing drugs exhausted Isabel. After each treatment, she felt so weak that she could barely move. She experienced the anticipated side effects of vomiting and hair loss. Once her hair began falling out in clumps, she went to the beauty parlor and had her head shaved. While some patients wore their baldness as a badge of courage, Isabel invested in a wig that was the same lush color as her own auburn hair. She had always considered her hair to be her best feature, and this wig - this nod to vanity - seemed a well-deserved comfort in light of her ordeal.

Alice drove her to and from her treatments. In order to spare George, Isabel slept in the guest room after each session at the hospital. Alice stayed in the twin bed beside her and was up with her during the night, holding her head as she vomited, washing her face and putting cold compresses on her forehead. Isabel would not let her telephone Dr. Stewart. She was unwilling to disturb him, although she found comfort in the knowledge that he had told her she could call him at any time.

Only once, toward the end of her therapy, did Isabel have a reaction so severe that Dr. Stewart had to be summoned, and Isabel was so ill at that point, with chills and a raging fever, that she had no say in the matter. Dr. Stewart had her admitted to the hospital, and when she woke feeling better at three in the morning, she found him sleeping in a chair beside her bed. When she stirred, he was instantly aware.

"It's so late," she whispered. "You must go home now. I'll be all right."

He stood beside her bed and took her hand. She brought his hand up and pressed it against her cheek.

"Thank you," she said, softly. "I can't thank you enough."

He leaned over and rested his other hand quietly on her shoulder. "I'm so proud of you, Isabel," he said. And she thought she heard him catch his breath as he spoke her name.

Isabel's therapy finally ended and her battle for remission was successful. Dr. Stewart smiled broadly as he gave her the good news. By the time of her next appointment, she had gained back some of the weight she had lost, and her hair was growing in. The fact that it was still very short was strangely becoming, giving her something of the look of a gamine.

When further tests showed there was no change in her remission, she said, "It was worth it - the chemotherapy, I mean. It was worth it to have this time. My family and I have just returned from two weeks on the Eastern Shore of Maryland. I would get up most mornings while everyone else was still asleep and take solitary walks on the beach with our dogs."

"Such walks are good for the soul," Dr. Stewart smiled.

"Exactly," Isabel replied.

"I want you to know that, in just over two weeks, I will be gone for five days. I'm going to a medical conference in Italy, in Venice. I've written the dates, the name of the hotel and the telephone number." He handed Isabel a slip of paper. "Dr. Gold will be covering for me while I'm away, and I've given you his number as well in case of an emergency. But I want to be sure that you know where to reach me."

"Thank you," Isabel said as she glanced at the piece of paper. "You'll be at the Hôtel des Bains on the Lido!"

"Yes, that's right. Do you know it?"

"Only for its literary associations. Thomas Mann used

it as the setting for *Death in Venice,* and the movie was filmed there. I believe it's very beautiful and very grand. I envy you staying there."

Duncan Stewart smiled warmly as they stood simultaneously, and the doctor came around the desk and offered her his hand. When she took it, he placed his other hand on top of hers. They looked at each other, and Isabel spontaneously leaned forward and gave him a hug, which he returned. She left quickly then, curiously flustered, and unable to think of anything further to say.

Two mornings later, Isabel had a dream just before waking that made clear to her something her conscious mind would not broach. In her dream, she and Dr. Stewart had fallen deeply in love with each other. When she woke, this feeling she had for him remained, and it frightened her. She struggled to rationalize it away. Women, she chided herself, often develop crushes on their physicians. A doctor, with the power he has to save or prolong lives is, after all, a sort of omnipotent father figure. She was obviously mistaking gratitude for love. She went on in this vein for some time, castigating herself and denying the truth of her feeling until she could reject it no longer.

She had to accept that, despite everything, she had fallen in love with him. Of course, she could never tell him. She had no way to gage what his reaction would be. Surely he would see her as some sort of blithering idiot. But even if, by some remote possibility, he should happen to return her feelings, what then? The idea of furtive afternoon liaisons in cheap motels or hotels, where she might easily be recognized by someone in George's congregation, made

WHILE THE MUSIC LASTS

the idea of an affair completely untenable. All of New Haven and its environs were not large enough to guarantee absolute safety and, without such a guarantee, she could never act. She had George and Emily and Alice to consider. It was of paramount importance that they never be hurt, and that meant that they could never know anything of what she was now feeling. All of these thoughts swirled in her head until it began to ache from the effort of trying to find some kind of resolution.

She lay on the sofa with her eyes closed. George was at the church. Emily was at school, and Alice, insisting that Isabel was not yet strong enough to do housework, had gone to the grocery store.

Slowly, one thought took hold in her mind: Italy. He was going to Italy. She could go there. But how could she explain Italy to her family? And how could she go there alone? She believed she had not yet recovered enough to travel so far on her own, and she knew George and Alice would never allow her to go without a companion.

Gradually a plan began to form that seemed so audacious that its very boldness might make it feasible. She would tell her family that she wanted to go to Italy, to Venice, as a sort of spiritual retreat. Venice was the city of artists and writers, the city she had always wanted to visit and that she had never seen. Venice was where she was supposed to have gone with her mother. Isabel could hear Duncan telling her that patients in remission sometimes did things they had always wanted to do. Well, this was what she wanted to do. She would be gone for five or six days at the most. Knowing she was not only rationalizing the situation but also conveniently putting aside the fact that she was thinking of adultery, she told herself that she was a special case. Surely, no one would begrudge a terminally ill person those few days in Venice.

Who would accompany her? She needed to be with someone she could trust completely, someone who would not ask her embarrassing questions. Under normal circumstances, Alice would be the logical choice, but now that was impossible. Then, suddenly, she knew. It would have to be Andrew.

From their childhood days, when they conspired against Miss Murphy, to the present, she and Andrew had been staunch friends. She knew he would do anything for her, especially now, since he was aware of her illness and of the fact that she had recently gone into remission.

Isabel took her cell phone, went upstairs, turned on the radio in the bedroom and locked herself in the bathroom. She dialed Andrew's number at his law office. He answered the phone himself.

"Isabel!" he said cordially, "how are you? And I mean that literally - how are you, really?"

"I'm still doing well, thank you. But I have a very great favor to ask. You will think I'm completely bonkers."

"No more than usual, surely," he teased. "Fire away."

"I hope you will accompany me on a flight to Venice, Italy, in a couple of weeks. I want to stay there for five or six days, and then you and I would return to the States together.

As far as George and Alice are concerned, you are going to Venice on business, and when you told me, I asked if I could go with you because it would give me an opportunity to see the city for the first time. Of course, I will explain things further to you, but I won't give many more details because I want you to have deniability. You can tell your wife you are doing this to fulfill the last wish of a deranged friend if you like - and swear her to secrecy."

There was silence at the other end of the phone as Andrew took all of this in. Finally, he said, "Since it's for you, of course I'll do it. But I don't understand. Why all of this cloak and dagger stuff? Have you got yourself hooked up with the CIA or something?" He sounded half serious.

"No, it's nothing like that, I promise. You will just have to trust me."

"Would you want me to stay in Venice with you the entire time?"

"No, not really. Why?"

"I have an old friend who has a house in Tuscany. He has been after me for ages to visit him. This would give me a chance to see him."

Isabel was amazed by this turn of events. She had been worried that Andrew might accidentally see her with Duncan Stewart. That possible problem now seemed to be solved. "It will be fine for you to stay with him, Andrew, really. Thank you so very much."

That evening, at supper, Isabel said, "I spoke with Andrew today. He's going on a business trip to Italy, Venice actually, in a couple of weeks and I've been thinking I might just go with him. I've always wanted to see Venice. I imagine it will be a good time of the year to be there after most of the summer tourists have left. Anyway, this is an opportunity, and I'd like to take it. Forgive me if it is selfish of me not to invite you to come along, but I see this almost as a sort of retreat, something I once was going to do with my mother and something I now need to do on my own."

George and Alice hesitated only briefly before they agreed that she should most certainly go. George asked, "How will you get back?"

WHILE THE MUSIC LASTS

"Oh, I'd only be in Venice for a few days; then, I'd fly home when Andrew does."

That settled the matter. Isabel felt a strong twinge of guilt and was reminded of a line in one of her favorite old, classic films, *Brief Encounter*, where Celia Johnson says something to the effect of "how easy it is to lie when you know you are trusted implicitly."

PART FIVE

somewhere i have never travelled, gladly beyond
any experience, your eyes have their silence:
in your most frail gesture are things which enclose me,
or which i cannot touch because they are too near

your slightest look easily will unclose me
though i have closed myself as fingers,
you open always petal by petal myself as Spring opens
(touching skilfully, mysteriously) her first rose

or if your wish be to close me, i and
my life will shut very beautifully, suddenly,
as when the heart of this flower imagines
the snow carefully everywhere descending;

nothing we are to perceive in this world equals
the power of your intense fragility: whose texture
compels me with the colour of its countries,
rendering death and forever with each breathing

(i do not know what it is about you that closes
and opens; only something in me understands
the voice of your eyes is deeper than all roses)
nobody, not even the rain, has such small hands

e.e. cummings

WHILE THE MUSIC LASTS

Dear Duncan,

You will remember from my medical history that I was once hospitalized for depression. What you do not know is why. I was, at the time, very much in love with a man who did not love me. He told me so quite bluntly. Just after this happened, my mother died suddenly and unexpectedly. The combination of these two events caused me to be hospitalized for four months.

When I was released, I made a vow that I would never again allow myself to love any man so deeply. I explained all of this to my husband before I married him. And I have kept that vow, until now. But, as much as I have fought it - and believe me, I have fought it - the truth is that I have fallen in love with you. I love your goodness. I love your gentleness. I love your kindness. I can say that, for the first time, I truly understand what Elizabeth Barrett Browning meant when she said of Robert Browning:

> I love thee to the depth and breadth and height
> My soul can reach, when feeling out of sight
> For the ends of Being and ideal Grace.

My first thought was to keep this love for you a secret. My husband, daughter and sister-in-law can never know any of what I am telling you because it would hurt them and I have absolutely no right to cause them pain. They have always wanted only what is best for me.

When you receive this letter, I will be staying in Venice at the Gritti Palace Hotel, and I will remain there for three days after your conference ends. If you think you can love me, please come to me there. If you care nothing for me, I beg you not to telephone or send a message. It would be incredibly difficult for me to hear or read your well-intentioned refusal.

If you should come out of some misguided sense of duty or, worse still, because you pity me, I will know - believe me, I will know. And that would cause far more harm to me than for you not to come at all.

I can accept silence from you. I can accept your absence. And I promise you that, whatever happens, I will do nothing to harm myself. I offer you, as insurance, how my family would react. I have traveled such a distance, in part, to assure that they will be protected. Their well-being is vital to me and I cannot jeopardize it. Also, after grappling with my own mortality these last months, I think I can take nearly anything now and not falter.

Yours,

Isabel Larsson

PART SIX

For most of us, there is only the unattended

Moment, the moment in and out of time,

The distraction fit, lost in a shaft of sunlight,

The wild thyme unseen, or the winter lightning

Or the waterfall, or music heard so deeply

That it is not heard at all, but you are the music

While the music lasts.

> T.S. Eliot
> The Dry Salvages
> *Four Quartets*

WHILE THE MUSIC LASTS

Drinks had been served and the flight attendants were readying the dinner carts. The trip so far – they were now two hours out of New York – had been uneventful. Andrew and Isabel had kept up a light-hearted banter typical of old friends who could relax in each other's company. On one or two occasions, Isabel noticed a protective expression of concern on Andrew's face.

The captain announced that there was possible turbulence ahead and advised passengers to remain in their seats with their seat belts fastened.

Isabel hesitated, and then, making a deliberate effort to keep her voice even, said, "Andrew, do you believe in heaven and hell and all of that?"

Andrew, realizing at once that this was more than just an idle query, paused before he answered. "I just don't know, Isabel," he said finally. "I'm not religious, but I like to think there might be a heaven, at least."

"Yes, so do I," Isabel responded.

They were quiet for several minutes before Andrew spoke again. "I think the universe and our place in it will always be beyond the limits of human understanding. We humans seem to be in the unique position of knowing that we do not know.

I once read an article in a scientific magazine, *Discover* I think it was, about what happened before the Big Bang. It seems some scientists are positing a theory that our universe exists on a three-dimensional membrane that is right next to another membrane. The other membrane may be just a photon away, but we can never see it. The Big Bang occurs when these membranes collide and matter starts expanding. We are now somewhere in the middle of such an expansion which will continue on and on until our universe is nearly empty. Then our universe's membrane will collide again with the other membrane and there will be another Big Bang. Creation and expansion will start over again and go on forever. So space and time are infinite."

"That is a fascinating theory," Isabel said.

"Yes, and I rather like it," Andrew smiled. "If there need to be two membranes to make the Big Bang, Freud would say..."

... "that has a sexual connotation." Isabel finished his sentence for him and they both laughed.

The lights in the cabin dimmed. They decided not to watch the in-flight movie, a thoroughly predictable adventure story. Isabel saw Andrew stifle a yawn.

"Please," she said, "try to get some sleep. You don't need to stay awake to keep me company."

"Are you sure?"

"Absolutely," Isabel said. "Will my reading light disturb you?"

"No, not in the least," Andrew murmured and closed his eyes.

Isabel took a copy of Elizabeth Barrett Browning's *Sonnets from the Portuguese* out of her bag. Isabel was aware that these poems had nothing to do with Portugal or the Portuguese language. Barrett Browning had used that title to disguise the fact that she was, in fact, writing about the passion she felt for Robert Browning.

After reading for about twenty minutes, Isabel put the book of poetry back in her purse and checked to see that the letter she had written for Duncan Stewart was safely in the bottom of her bag, underneath her passport. It had been foolhardy of her to write to him while she was still at home with George and Emily. But one night, unable to sleep, and very excited about her plan to go to Italy she went

WHILE THE MUSIC LASTS

downstairs, took up a pen and poured out her thoughts to him. She almost burned the letter but was afraid that she might never again be able to say, in quite the same way, all that it contained. So she had deposited it in the very bottom of her bag where it remained.

She switched off her light and saw her reflection in the window as she stared out at the vast darkness of sky and sea. She listened to the monotonous roar of the jet's engines and thought, "If creation repeats over and over again, my molecules might one day be part of another sentient being, and the billions of years between consciousness would pass as if they were part of only one night."

She knew she was tired and falling into the vague state between waking and sleeping because she thought she heard a voice, obviously from within her own head, saying, "What if, next time, you are not born at the top of the food chain?"

She reclined her seat and put the little airline pillow between herself and the window. She thought of Duncan Stewart and let the love she felt for him wash over her obliterating everything else.

The day continued to be bright and warm with a gentle breeze. Isabel decided to sit outside on the vaporetto going to the Lido, that narrow bit of land that shields Venice from the open sea. Her heart was pounding. She believed the next hour would be the most dangerous of her entire trip. She was convinced, irrationally, that if Duncan Stewart saw her and recognized her before he received her letter, that would be a very bad omen. She could almost hear him saying, "What are you doing here?" And, if he said that, how could she reply? "Oh, I'm just a woman of loose morals who has decided to throw herself at you?" Isabel shivered momentarily and whispered, "Please God, don't let him see me!"

Taxis were waiting near the vaporetto stop and Isabel hailed one.

"I want to go to the Grand Hôtel des Bains, please, And I will need you to wait for me while I deliver a letter to the desk clerk. Do you understand?"

"Yes, good. I wait."

As the taxi carried her ever closer to her destination, Isabel was half aware of elegant shops, tree-lined streets, villas and gardens. Finally the car stopped at the entrance of the imposing nineteenth-century hotel.

Isabel pulled her coat around her and reached for her letter. She would have no time to fumble for it in her purse once she was inside. She also reiterated that the taxi driver should wait for her; she could not take the chance of being stranded in this place.

"Yes. Yes. I wait," the driver said.

Isabel walked briskly into the lobby. A woman in front of her had engaged the clerk's attention. Isabel heard her ask for directions. The clerk produced a map from beneath the desk, and he and the woman bent their heads over it, studying it.

Isabel's knees began to tremble. "Hurry up!" she thought. "Oh, God, I have to get out of here!"

After an agonizing few minutes, the woman thanked the clerk and he turned his attention to Isabel.

"Yes, Madame?"

"You have a Dr. Duncan Stewart staying here, I believe?"

The clerk ran his finger down the names on the

register.

"Yes, Madame. You wish me to ring his room to let him know you are here?"

"No!" Isabel said in a tone she was afraid sounded almost like a shout. Lowering her voice, she said, "No, that won't be necessary. But please see that he gets this letter." Her hands were shaking as she handed it to him. "It's important."

"Very good, Madame."

"It's terribly important."

"Yes, Madame, I am putting it in his box now."

"Thank you," Isabel said as she turned and fled.

She directed the driver to take her back to the vaporetto. He, perhaps hoping for a larger tip, became suddenly loquacious.

"The Venice Film Festival is held in that building," he said. "And there is the Grand Hotel Excelsior…"

Isabel tried to be polite, murmuring the necessary replies. But her thoughts were concentrated on just one thing: leaving the Lido.

Back at the Piazza San Marco, still tense from her excursion to the Hôtel des Bains, Isabel decided to walk for a while before returning to her hotel. She was window-shopping on a side street when she saw a tiny oil painting in the window of one of the little shops. At first she could not believe what it was. Entering the store, she asked the proprietor to remove the picture from the window so she could examine it more closely. It was a copy of the head of Dante Gabriel Rossetti's *Blessed Damozel.* Isabel could see his name on the back. The study showed the stars in the Blessed Damozel's hair but, since the detail was only of the head, her hands holding the three lilies were missing.

WHILE THE MUSIC LASTS

Isabel asked the price and bought the little oil knowing she was paying too much for it. But the price was of no consequence: if Duncan Stewart came, she would be able to give it to him. She began to think of the evening she had first met him when he had told her that she reminded him of the painting. Had the poem and the picture, in some way, foretold her present situation? If there was a heaven, and if she was going there, she would indeed want him to be there with her. But the Blessed Damozel's wish had been thwarted... and Poe's poem *The Raven*, was an anguished expression of grief.

It was only then that Isabel abruptly confronted what her death might mean to Duncan Stewart. She started to have second thoughts about telling him her feelings. She began to think that she had been incredibly self-indulgent. She wanted this doctor who had been so good and kind to her to come to her in Venice purely for her own sake... and for very selfish reasons. She wanted him to love her, and she wanted all of this without really thinking through what it could do to him.

He had once been desperately hurt according to Ed Marsden. Now, if he should, in fact, love her, was she not just setting him up to be hurt again? How could she, who knew only too well what grief could do, take responsibility for inflicting it on someone she loved?

Walking faster, she passed an English language bookshop which had a copy of Thomas Mann's *Death in Venice* on a small cart outside. Anger at her own actions peaked and she began muttering to herself, "This is not some novel you are playing at here. This is a man's life you are dealing with, a man who will probably survive you by many years. You want some absurd, melodramatic love scene, some ridiculous Hollywood ending; you might as well hire violins to play maudlin music in the background! If he loves you, you are condemning him to mourn for you. Is that what you want, you stupid, selfish woman?"

Isabel was distraught. It was too late to recall her letter. She would have to see it through. She hoped that he would not care and that he might not come. That night, the little sleep she got was restless and filled with ugly dreams where strangers were taunting her and mocking her.

She rose early and asked to have some tea and croissants sent up which, subsequently, she did not touch. She was still in her room at eleven trying to focus on the furniture and the architecture, anything so that she would not have to acknowledge the painful, rhythmic throbbing in her head and the question she asked herself over and over: "You fool, what have you done?"

It was just before noon when she heard a quiet knock on her door. She opened it and found Duncan Stewart standing there before her. She backed up as he entered the room and closed the door behind him.

He started to speak but she kept moving away from him and shaking her head saying, "Please forgive me. I have no right... no... I'm so sorry!"

He stopped walking toward her, and he seemed confused. "I don't understand. Why are you sorry? What's wrong?" His face went pale as he attempted to grasp the situation. "You've changed your mind," he said at length, looking down. "That's it, isn't it? You don't love me really... you've come to your senses." He set his jaw as if to steel himself against this truth but his shoulders slumped and he could not conceal his utter dejection.

Isabel had not anticipated seeing him like this, and at that moment all she knew was that she had to comfort him. She ran to him.

WHILE THE MUSIC LASTS

He saw her approaching and he reached for her, holding her close as she blurted out, "Duncan, I love you so much! I can't help loving you, and I can't hide it... But don't you see what I've done? When I'm gone, I'll be leaving you to grieve and that's unforgivable. I know a lot about grief and -"

"Oh, darling," Duncan said, "you don't understand do you? You have nothing to reproach yourself for. I loved you long before you sent your letter. I think I have loved you from the beginning. . ." He held her face gently between his hands. "So the grief would be there in any event."

Isabel wanted desperately to believe what he was saying but feared he was simply trying to console her. "Have you cared for me that long?" she whispered. "Have you, really?"

"Yes," he replied, "absolutely." He smiled at her, and she could see the love for her in his eyes. "Let's not think about the future. We have each other now and, remember, that's more than many people have in a lifetime."

Relief overcame her as she leaned against him.

He held her then with infinite tenderness and, as his lips sought hers, he began to lead her to a place she had never been before and to carry her with him to heights she never knew she could attain. Later, as they lay quietly on the bed, holding each other, the tears on her face were tears of joy.

They had lunch on the terrace of the Gritti Palace. The day was glorious with a cloudless sky and temperatures in the seventies. The maitre d'hotel took them to a table set with blue linens close to the Grand Canal. The blue and

WHILE THE MUSIC LASTS

white awning overhead rippled in the gentle breeze. Next to them was a large party of British tourists, ten people in all. The women wore elegant dresses and hats and the men were in suits. Isabel and Duncan knew some festive occasion was involved. Just what it was became obvious when dessert was served and the assembled company burst into song: "Happy birthday, dear Fiona. Happy birthday to you!"

Isabel brought a small package wrapped in string to lunch and presented it to Duncan between the first course and the entrée.

"For me?" he said. "What on earth?" He slipped off the paper and revealed the small painting of the head of the *Blessed Damozel.* "Oh, Isabel!" he said astounded. "I'm touched beyond measure. I will always cherish this." He reached for her hand to thank her. They continued holding hands and marveling at the view.

"Have you been to Florian's?" Duncan asked.

"No, but I've read about it. It's the café that's famous for being the haunt of artists and writers: Balzac and Shelley and..."

Duncan nodded and smiled at her. "Let me take you there for dessert," he said.

They went to St. Mark's Square and found the café that advertised it had been in the same location since 1720. They decided to sit inside so they could study the murals under glass of Arab men and women, probably done in the nineteenth century. They sat in a corner near the window on little chairs with red plush seats and with a small white marble table in front of them. Isabel ordered a hot chocolate and Duncan ordered the same with the addition of whipped cream and a biscuit on his.

Just outside the window, a band played various

WHILE THE MUSIC LASTS

selections and was presently giving a rendition of *The Blue Danube*. A small grey-haired lady in a beige fall coat stopped and danced by herself to the waltz. When the piece was finished she spoke to all of the band members, smiling and gesticulating happily. Isabel thought she must be reliving some happy moment from her youth. They each gave her a hug before she moved on.

A Japanese tourist peered through the window at them, saw them holding hands and smiled at them, giving them a thumbs-up sign. Everyone seemed to be in a good mood and Isabel wondered if she was looking at the world through the prism of her own joy. She could scarcely believe that she was sitting in this café with a man she adored and who loved her in return.

Duncan told her that he had to be back to the Lido before dinner because he was the evening's featured speaker. But they would have tomorrow and the next day. They talked until the shadows were lengthening, and Isabel looked at her watch, worried that Duncan was not allowing enough time for his return. "I'll walk you to the vaporetto," she said.

"No," he said, "I'll take you back to your hotel and get a water taxi from there."

"A water taxi? But those are so expensive!"

"Everything today should be special, don't you agree?" he asked, beaming at her.

She stood with him on the dock before he got into the taxi. "Tomorrow we'll ride in a gondola," he said.

"Oh, yes, please! That will be wonderful," she answered.

Then, in front of the hotel staff and the water-taxi driver, he took her in his arms and kissed her.

He sat in the back of the boat where he could see her,

WHILE THE MUSIC LASTS

and she smiled and waved until he was out of sight.

She walked into her room and went to the vanity table and sat down. Turning on the small lamp, she gazed at her reflection in the mirror. Her eyes were dancing and her lips were curved in a smile. Twilight became night and she scarcely noticed. Finally she rose, put on her nightgown and stretched out on the bed. Her hand caressed the spot where Duncan Stewart had lain beside her.

Isabel had never known such serenity. As she was beginning to fall asleep, she dreamed she was standing on the green bank of the Susquehanna, clutching her mother's hand. Suddenly no longer afraid, she let go and, stepping forward, she allowed herself to be drawn, very gently, into the endless flow of the river.

ACKNOWLEDGEMENTS

It is a pleasure to thank my editor, Andrew Clyde Little, and his wife Dolce for their invaluable assistance. I am also grateful to my copy editor, Claire Whitehill, for her excellent and meticulous work.

The following people read the manuscript and gave me their suggestions and support: Joan Bannister, Marcia Bures, Gomer and Betty Anne Davies, Eve Feldman, Holly Richards Frost, Thomas and Mary Ellen Frost, Evelyn Hughes, and Nancy Swearer. I am indebted to all of them.

Charlotte Blandford was very helpful in storing several drafts on her computer and typing the finished manuscript.

Finally, I am most grateful to my husband for his unwavering enthusiasm and encouragement.

Cover design and author photograph by Andrew Clyde Little.

The use of The Blessed Damozel by Dante Gabriel Rossetti is by permission of the Fogg Museum, Harvard University.

The use of *Four Quartets* by T.S. Eliot is by permission of Harcourt Brace.

The use of *somewhere i have never travelled, gladly beyond* by e.e. cummings is by permission of Liveright.

Susan K. Frost received a degree in English literature from the College of William and Mary where she won first prize for poetry in the literary journal. She did graduate work at Yale and Columbia Universities. Ms. Frost lived for many years in Pennsylvania where her husband was on the faculty of Swarthmore College. Their son is a lawyer in Washington, D.C. Ms. Frost has published articles in the *Maryland Magazine* and *The Swarthmorean*. She traveled extensively in Europe and Asia and has lived in England and Hawaii. She and her husband now divide their time between New Hampshire and Florida.

ISBN 142510142-9

Edwards Brothers Malloy
Oxnard, CA USA
September 15, 2015